5655

Schizophrenia

Schizophrenia

by Douglas W. Smith

Franklin Watts
New York • Chicago • London • Toronto • Sydney
A Venture Book

Photographs copyright ©: Monkmeyer Press Photo/Grunnitus: p. 1;
North Wind Picture Archives, Alfred, ME: pp. 2 left, 3 top;
The Bettmann Archive: pp. 3 bottom, 4;
Rainbow/Kim Massie: pp. 5, 7;
Photo Researchers, Inc./Stan Goldblatt: p. 6;
Mary Ellen Mark/Library: pp. 10, 11, 12, 13, 14, 15, 16.

Library of Congress Cataloging-in-Publication Data

Smith, Douglas W. (Douglas Wayne), 1949–
Schizophrenia / by Douglas W. Smith.
p. cm. — (A Venture book)
Includes bibliographical references and index.
Summary: Describes the nature, causes, and treatment of this
common type of mental illness.
ISBN 0-531-12514-9
1. Schizophrenia—Juvenile literature. [1. Schizophrenia.
2. Mental illness.]   I. Title.
RC514.S548   1992
616.89′82—dc20   92-21140 CIP AC

Contents

Introduction
9

1
What Is "Normal"?
11

2
Schizophrenia:
A Mental Illness in Perspective
19

3
What Characterizes Schizophrenia?
31

4
What Causes Schizophrenia?
42

5
Treating Schizophrenia
50

6
Two Case Studies of Schizophrenia
64

7
Schizophrenia:
Past, Present, and Future
71

Organizations to Contact
for Further Information
80

Source Notes
82

Glossary
85

For Further Reading
92

Index
93

This book is dedicated to my dad.
For the encouragement
and help in writing
over three decades. . . .
and for the genes to go with it.

Introduction

Human beings are complicated creatures. Physically, we resemble our evolutionary ancestors. Many of our internal organs are nearly identical to those of other species. Our hearts, muscles, bones, and eyes have the same functions as those in most mammals.

One feature sets humans apart from the other animals: the human mind. Our brains are well developed in ways that the brains of most other animals are not. The mental ability to reason and solve intricate problems distinguishes human beings from other animals of equal physical complexity. Understanding, and showing emotion are also distinctly human. But this evolutionary novelty comes with a dark side.

Just as disease or injury can cause physical illness, disruption of the human mind can cause mental illness. Mental as well as physical systems of human beings can go awry. Our understanding of mental illness is much less clear than our understanding of many physical ailments. We can easily understand what causes chicken pox because we can isolate and see the culprit that causes the disease under a microscope. On the other hand, it is usually not as easy to understand what specifically causes an illness of the mind. Although there are better clues every year from our scientific investigations, the complex human mind remains poorly understood.

Schizophrenia is one common type of mental illness, affecting many millions of people throughout the world. In recent years, scientists have begun to understand more about the possible causes, predisposing factors, types, and possible treatments for schizophrenia. Learning more about schizophrenia will be an intellectual investment well spent, and will provide a better knowledge about very important aspects of human behavior.

A Note About Terminology

A disease can and should be separated from the person who has it. Diseases are seen as foreign enemies that invade the body. When we get a cold or the flu or an ulcer, or cancer, or diabetes, we say that we *have* those diseases. Treating schizophrenia as a disease in the same way makes good sense. It is both accurate and sensitive.

Sometimes we hear the term for the *disease* used to describe the *person,* as in the word *schizophrenic.* This is improper. It is preferable to say that a person "has schizophrenia" rather than to call someone a schizophrenic.

1

What Is "Normal"?

Gerald is a twenty-three-year-old man who is constantly suspicious and frightened. He is afraid that most people are "out to get him" and trusts few people. He has no close friends. He cannot hold a job for more than a few days because he is unable to concentrate on or cope with even simple tasks or to interact appropriately with the people with whom he works.

He is even afraid of his own senses. His skin prickles, his head seems to constantly hum, and he hears voices that annoy him. Unpleasant odors choke him. His food has no taste. Bright and colorful visions pass before his eyes, ranging from brilliant butterflies to bloody body parts. The clinking of ice in a nearby pitcher seems to him to be part of a device trying to destroy him.

When someone talks to him, Gerald hears only disconnected words. These words often touch off an old memory or a strange dream. Instead of *listening, he finds his attention wandering from his inner thoughts and he focuses on the grotesque way the speaker moves his mouth or the loud scrape his chair makes against the floor. Gerald cannot understand what the person is trying to tell him, or why.*

When Gerald tries to speak, his own words sound foreign to him. Broken phrases tumble out of his mouth over and over and over again. Inside he is frightened and worried all the time. He sometimes thinks about killing himself.

Approximately fifty million people on our planet suffer the way Gerald does. They have *schizophrenia*. It is obvious that Gerald's thoughts, perceptions, and emotions are disorganized. His withdrawal from social contacts is not how normal human beings live. He has a warped sense of what the real world offers, and this view makes life very uncomfortable for him. Because of his schizophrenia, Gerald does not appropriately process a good deal of information—sights, sounds, and other sensations—from the world around him, in the way that most of us do constantly without even thinking about it.

To understand how and why persons with schizophrenia are affected by their disease, and how their behavior, thoughts, and feelings are different, it is important to explore what we mean by the concept of "normal."

"Normal"—A Simple Word, But Not Easy To Define

The words *normal* and *abnormal* are used to describe everything from weather patterns to instrument indications on a car or plane to people. But what do these words mean as applied to the complicated issues of schizophrenia?

The word *normal* means "conforming with an accepted standard, model, or pattern." It can also mean the "average" of a large group, for example, in type, appearance, achievement, function, or development. Normal suggests "regular" or "standard." The word *abnormal* simply means just the opposite. Abnormal is not normal, or is "away from what is considered normal."

In describing "normal" weather patterns, for example, we all have a sense of what that means. "Hot, humid, and hazy" describes normal weather for a day in July for the northern hemisphere. A freak snowstorm in summer is abnormal weather, as is a heat wave in January. Notice that deciding what is normal versus abnormal has something to do with our expectations.

The temperature and oil pressure gauges of a car, truck, or airplane usually operate in the "normal" range. That is, their readings ordinarily fall within accepted limits for the engine's operation. If something goes wrong, the gauge will indicate an *abnormal* reading, which should alert the driver or pilot that the engine's function is *no longer standard or regular*, and that more problems may occur.

Individual people can also be termed normal and abnormal. However, such labels must be used with caution. Hastily labeling people with words like *weird, freaky, strange,* or *abnormal* not only may hurt their feelings, but also might earmark them wrongly for a long time. A proper diagnosis of any illness is accomplished by professionals using "standards" accumulated over many years of observation and investigation. Defining normal is far from a simple process. In the health professions, much effort goes into insuring that the definitions of normal and abnormal for many activities and conditions are both precise and useful.

Why Use The Terms Normal And Abnormal At All?

As they evolved on this planet, human beings have developed complex reasoning skills. Members of early communities, such as cave dwellers, over centuries of common agreement among themselves, began to decide what is normal. That is, the talent of early humans for thinking and analysis led them to decide what they themselves would accept as normal behavior or conduct. Such decisions may be quite arbitrary, and may mean only choices of actions and language that have been agreed upon by the community.

The guidelines for living and behaving were passed down through the ages and changed with time. Today there are certainly ample amounts of written and unwritten normal standards for our times. All societies, in fact, have quite detailed rules and principles by which their members live.

Some rules may deal with behaviors that are quite surprising to us. For example, certain tribes in the highlands of New Guinea still pierce holes through their noses and wear jewelry made of animal bone. They also carve decorative tattoos into their skin with sharp instruments. For clothing they wear only loincloths or brief coverings made from grass, walk barefoot, and carry spears.

In that society, these customs are normal; they represent standard, regular behavior. In fact, this behavior is not only acceptable, it is *expected* of each member of the tribe. But what is normal for this small, isolated society, would not be normal for a large city in North America. Imagine what would happen if a New Guinea tribesman were to stroll down the main street of a large city, painted and scarred, covered only by some grass, barefoot, with bones through his nose and a long spear in hand. If we all knew that this person had actually just arrived from New Guinea, we might be tolerant, if not curious. But such behavior would not be *expected* unless it occurred in a parade or some special event.

It is more likely that we would interpret such an unusual sight as *abnormal*. This person would appear abnormal because his clothing was not standard to the large group of people in North American cities.

Now reverse the scene. Imagine a businessman in a three-piece suit and tie, with a leather briefcase and wingtip shoes, setting out to hunt wild boars in the highlands of New Guinea with the tribesman just described. Without a doubt, tribal members would find the city slicker's outfit abnormal and inappropriate, if not hilarious!

We can now understand that clothing, jewelry, and grooming habits considered normal in some societies would be very abnormal in others. These are not value judgments made on one culture by another, but rather decisions made by each culture individually. Objections to using the words normal and abnormal are heard from time to time. Until more useful terms are developed, however, they are very much a part of the language used to discuss mental illness.

How "Normal" And "Abnormal" Apply To The Human Mind

If normal means standard or regular or expected when we speak of the weather or someone's clothing, what does it mean when we speak of a person's thoughts, actions, or feelings? All of us have millions of thoughts in our lifetimes. How do we know whether they are normal or abnormal?

The thinking that takes place in the human mind is both powerful and private. But if no contact exists with other members of the society there is no way to determine what is normal. To make such a determination, thinking or behavior must be revealed through speech or actions by an individual, and observed by others. The observer can then judge whether or not the thoughts, statements, or actions are appropriate.

If the behavior or language is deemed appropriate, it will be considered normal. If it shows weird, bizarre, or inappropriate thinking, feelings, or actions, it will be judged abnormal. Human survival over time has to some extent depended upon societies developing community guidelines of acceptable behavior, rather than allowing every person to simply behave in his or her own individual way.

Are The Lines Between Normal And Abnormal Always Clear?

Every human being may act in unusual or abnormal ways at times. But is this abnormal behavior? Perhaps, but it may be acceptable because it occurs at a costume party, or is exhibited by someone who is reacting with anger or disappointment to a bad test grade, or with grief following the loss of a friend. In other words, a little strange behavior is usually allowed, as long as there is an accompanying reason that is also obvious. Most of the time, other people observing such behavior also know that the abnormal behavior is temporary and deliberate, and can be stopped at a moment's notice.

Abnormal acting or thinking which may be linked to a specific cause, or does not last very long, is called *acute*. Quite often alcohol or drugs can lead to abnormal behavior that is termed acute, because it is short-lived. The occurrence of abnormal behavior does not automatically mean a person is mentally unstable. The conditions, the time, the place, and especially how long the behavior lasts and how much it impairs the person's ability to function, are all important to deciding how serious the strange behavior really is.

Statistics Help To Sort
Normal From Abnormal

A sharp dividing line between normal and abnormal behavior, thinking, or feeling simply does not exist. Behaviors of all kinds, in any individual, tend to blend together. However, scientists have developed ways to distinguish differences through the use of *statistics,* which are the numerical expressions of collections of information. These numbers can be plotted to form a curve or graph which visually displays a clearer view of the way in which the population can be divided into normal and abnormal individuals.

If we collected data on people, and grouped symbols (one for each person) as to their position with respect to normal, the graph would be what is known as a *bell curve.* People who can be described as normal are the most numerous and make up the central cluster of symbols. Fewer and fewer people can be classified as more and more abnormal and are shown as fewer symbols toward the far edges of the curve.

The curve that can be drawn over these symbols represents a *normal distribution* for almost any trait within a defined population, such as human beings.

Simply stated, the shape of the curve—sharply downward on both sides—indicates that fewer and fewer people behave in ways that are more and more different from those of average or normal people. Finally, the point where the curve touches the baseline represents the end range of human behavior. In other words, nobody behaves in ways that are farther from normal than that point!

Schizophrenia, according to the normal distribution, is characterized by behavior which is a long way from how normal people act, think, feel, and talk. The actual numbers of people are relatively small in the total population, because they fall under the far edges of the distribution curve.

The concept of normal distribution is used in all facets of science. Height, weight, skin temperature, and blood pressure are examples of other items that can be distributed in a similar manner. As before, most of the population will be bunched under the middle range, with fewer and fewer people to either side as their departure from normal or average increases.

In the next chapter we will examine the special and usually very specific kinds of behavior, thinking, or feelings that make a person mentally ill.

Schizophrenia: A Mental Illness in Perspective

How far from the normal range behavior or feelings must be in order to be considered schizophrenia (pronounced skitz-oh-FREE-n-ee-uh), has also been defined by society. Over the years, mental health professionals have agreed upon a definition that is pretty clear: When a person's thinking, feeling, and behaving are so far from normal so as to interfere with his or her ability to function in everyday life, and delusions, hallucinations, or irregular thinking or emotions are produced, then he or she has a mental illness called schizophrenia.

If the various elements in this definition seem vague or complicated, they are! Understanding schizophrenia requires new vocabulary and understanding of new concepts from the field of mental sciences. Certain definitions are critical to a full understanding of the disease.

A delusion is a false and unreal belief. Although the belief seems very real to the person who has the delusion, it is absolutely not true. The delusional person accepts and lives with these beliefs as a part of his or her world. Such delusions would, of course, appear make-believe to other persons.

Hallucinations are somewhat like delusions, but the person who has hallucinations is not just thinking and living in a make-believe world, but goes one step farther. He or she actually believes that the imaginary sights or sounds are entirely real. Furthermore, persons afflicted with hallucinations may speak or act in response to these imaginary sights and sounds.

Normal thinking is usually orderly and organized. A person with schizophrenia, on the other hand, often thinks bizarre, inappropriate, and disorganized thoughts. The thoughts may be imaginary, far-fetched delusions, usually so weird that they make no sense whatever to another person. When a person with this kind of jumbled thinking speaks, the speech is out of order, off the subject, and perhaps impossible to follow. Often the person repeats things over and over again that, to an observer, don't mean anything.

Emotions (feelings) play a big role in schizophrenia. Most people respond appropriately, and more or less normally, to both words and actions. If something happy or funny happens, they may smile or laugh. Hearing sad or scary words may make people frown, or perhaps even cry.

Not so for the person with schizophrenia. Schizophrenia disturbs the emotional feelings that occur inside a person, and they respond inappropriately. For example, patients afflicted with schizophrenia may laugh or smile at pictures of rather gruesome subjects such as people being tortured. Such a reaction is hardly a normal or standard response. Reactions to other situations may be simply "flat" or lacking any sign of emotion. Inappropriate emotions are easily recognized not only by professionals but also by friends and acquaintances, because they are ill-adapted, ill-suited, ill-timed, and above all, improper. Such behavior also usually causes people nearby to feel uncomfortable, too.

Defining Schizophrenia

Behavioral scientists have recorded the behavior of thousands and thousands of people who do not think or act normally. Because schizophrenia is a complicated and serious disease, medical doctors must study the ailment for years to be able to accurately diagnose it. For several hundred years now, scientists who study people have gathered information and discussed case studies. Volumes have been written about abnormal behavior. Within the past fifty years, thousands of professionals worldwide who treat and study individuals with abnormalities in thinking, feeling, and behavior have brought their opinions and ideas together to share and discuss. The result has been the publication of a manual, called the Diagnostic and Statistical Manual of Mental Disorders, Third Edition, (Revised), known in the mental health profession simply as "DSM-III-R." This book contains both descriptions of the disease, as well as handy checklists of all the clues that confirm the diagnosis. The reference handbook allows medical doctors everywhere to diagnose schizophrenia (and all other mental illness) according to the same standards.

Most professionals refer to the diagnostic manual because it provides guidelines to aid diagnosis by, for example, listing the generally agreed-upon criteria[1] for the diagnosis of a specific mental illness such as schizophrenia. As researchers obtain more data every year on schizophrenia, the information in the manual is updated. So how we define schizophrenia today may be different just a few years from now. Unlike some concepts in science, the social sciences do not always have firm laws or principles to follow. Psychology and psychiatry, the disciplines that deal most directly with schizophrenia, are dynamic, changing fields. The amount of research undertaken each year to improve our understanding of this difficult disease is staggering, in terms of both time and money.

The diagnostic criteria used today may not be as relevant in a few years. For now, some guidelines appear to be fixed. A most important point that scientists agree upon in deciding when a person is afflicted by schizophrenia is: *If an individual is out of touch with reality and his or her thinking or behavior is different enough from "normal" so as to make coping with everyday life very difficult or impossible, then the person is suffering from schizophrenia.*

Neurosis and Psychosis

On the way to defining schizophrenia, we need to stop to define two more terms: *neurosis* and *psychosis*. The distinction between these two categories of mental illness are important if we are to understand just where schizophrenia fits in.

Neurosis (also called *psychoneurosis*) is also a form of mental illness. Some of its features seem similar to schizophrenia, but it is a different category of mental disorder. People with neurosis are anxious, worried, threatened, and distressed over situations that would not distress most of us. The neurosis makes them tend to avoid problems rather than cope with them. The behavior of persons with neurosis is maladaptive. That is, they are not clever or resourceful at dealing with personal and emotional turmoil, or at resolving emotional issues. They usually are self-defeating, feel inadequate, and are overly guilt-ridden. Neurosis brings an uncomfortable, miserable, unhealthy existence to millions of people.

For all the bad things neurosis brings its sufferers, there is one vitally important feature that it does not bring. Neurosis does *not* involve gross distortion of reality (delusions or hallucinations), or a major breakdown of thinking or emotions. In short, neurosis is a less serious mental disorder, although it may bring suffering that can be considered severe.

Psychosis, on the other hand, is a much more serious disorder. Psychosis is the scientific group name for extreme forms of mental disturbances, often called "insanity." There are several types of psychosis, but all have common features that are so severe that the individual is at times not capable of getting along in society. Now it's time to take a closer look at these features as we build a more detailed definition of schizophrenia.

Schizophrenia is a psychosis. Because schizophrenia causes its victim to lose touch with reality and to lose ability to function in society, it is one of the most serious of all the mental illnesses. Schizophrenia has the following specific symptoms or features that distinguish it from other psychoses:

- delusions and hallucinations
- disturbed emotions and thinking
- poor or no functioning in work, social relations, self-care
- decreased functioning continues for at least 6 months
- no known cause (especially not a physical cause such as drugs or brain tumors)

Other associated features can be:

- abnormal physical activity (pacing, rocking)
- abnormal speech and communication (silly talk, repetition)

- inappropriate manners, illogical ideas, bizarre behavior

In the diagnostic manuals, schizophrenia is broken down into a number of specific kinds, all of which have the features or symptoms listed above. More detailed descriptions of the various categories can help people who treat schizophrenia do a better job. Professionals who treat the disease are then better able to describe the behavior of their patients to others. The more precisely mental illness can be diagnosed, the better the professional treatment can be provided. Let's take a look at the three major types of schizophrenia that have been found.

Specific Types Of Schizophrenia

CATATONIC SCHIZOPHRENIA. Catatonic individuals have a condition that resembles suspended animation. They exhibit a loss of voluntary motion, and their arms or legs may hold any position in which they are placed. The person may slow down or stop completely. They may stand or sit endlessly in what is called a catatonic "stupor." (See Figure 1.)

Sometimes the catatonic person is rigid and difficult to move. Other times he or she may be highly excited, and flail around for no apparent reason. During periods of catatonic stupor or excitement, these individuals need help to prevent them from injuring themselves or others. The catatonic condition was more common in the past. Through the use of newer medications, it is very rare today.

DISORGANIZED SCHIZOPHRENIA. All schizophrenia patients, by definition, show some disorganization in their thinking and behavior. But there are many levels of disorganized thinking. Disorganized schizophre-

Figure 1. Symptoms of Two Types of Schizophrenia
(from DSM-III-R)

Diagnostic criteria for 295.2x Catatonic Type

A type of schizophrenia in which the clinical picture is dominated by any of the following:

(1) catatonic stupor (marked decrease in reactivity to the environment and/or reduction in spontaneous movements and activity) or mutism

(2) catatonic negativism (an apparently motiveless resistance to all instructions or attempts to be moved)

(3) catatonic rigidity (maintenance of a rigid posture against efforts to be moved)

(4) catatonic excitement (excited motor activity, apparently purposeless and not influenced by external stimuli)

(5) catatonic posturing (voluntary assumption of inappropriate or bizarre postures)

Diagnostic criteria for 295.3x Paranoid Type

A type of schizophrenia in which there are:

A. Preoccupation with one or more systematized delusions or with frequent auditory hallucinations related to a single theme.

B. None of the following: incoherence, marked loosening of associations, flat or grossly inappropriate affect, catatonic behavior, grossly disorganized behavior.

Specify stable type if criteria A and B have been met during all past and present active phases of the illness.

nia refers to people with very, or "grossly," disorganized behavior. These individuals additionally all exhibit highly inappropriate emotions. They show odd behavior, including facial grimaces, extreme withdrawal from other people, and continuous complaints about their health. An older term for this severe form of the disease is *hebephrenic schizophrenia*. The pattern of the illness is always identified by such things as hallucinations, absurd delusions, senseless laughter, and silliness. The term "hebephrenia" is still used in some parts of the world, and in the international classification system.

PARANOID-TYPE SCHIZOPHRENIA. Paranoid individuals focus their delusions or hallucinations on a single theme or idea. For example, a patient may believe that he or she is some famous person, either dead or alive, and may act like that person or have conversations with that person in their imaginary world. Sometimes persons with Paranoid-Type Schizophrenia will become angry, argue a lot, or even become violent. Whereas the behavior of the catatonic and disorganized types of schizophrenia is disorganized, persons with paranoid-type schizophrenia instead have highly organized imaginary worlds in which they live. Paranoid individuals are often anxious and frightened that something or someone is "out to get them." They often build fantastic and complex fantasy schemes about imaginary enemies.

Other diagnostic categories of schizophrenia exist, but are rare and less important. They exist principally for health-care providers to diagnose and sort out individuals who have unclear symptoms of the disease.

Is Schizophrenia The Same Around The World?

Schizophrenia is the same around the world, wherever one lives. For example, some New Guinea tribesmen, born and raised in their villages, have behavior that would be considered by their own clan to be abnormal. They might not call their abnormal behavior schizophrenia, but a person with the disease nevertheless displays the same symptoms of delusions, bizarre behavior, and so on, as does a person with schizophrenia living in New York City. Schizophrenia is observed and recorded within all cultures in every corner of the world. How this was discovered and how the disease differs within different cultures is a fascinating story of international effort.

In 1973, the World Health Organization published a study of people with schizophrenia around the world. The study asked: If all countries used the same set of standards (or criteria), would schizophrenia look the same everywhere? The results of the study were clear. Whether living in places like China, Columbia, Czechoslovakia, Nigeria, the United Kingdom, the Soviet Union or the United States, individuals with schizophrenia showed these symptoms: lack of insight, suspiciousness, false ideas, emotional dullness, poor relationships and communication, auditory hallucinations.[2]

This important discovery allowed scientists around the world to agree on a definition of schizophrenia. The results correspond to the general definition of schizophrenia presented at the beginning of this chapter, and support the detailed criteria specific to the various types of schizophrenia. With definitions in place, scientists could then study the history of the disease and work together to pool their information toward researching both a cause and a cure for schizophrenia.

A Brief History Of Schizophrenia

Mental illness has been reported since early recorded history, although it was not well defined until recently. It is not clear if schizophrenia, as we define it today, was as prevalent in times past as it is now. However, evidence that it probably existed is found scattered throughout literature and history. Terms like "madness," "mania," and "insane" were used long ago. For centuries, people who exhibited strange and unexplainable behavior were sometimes considered "possessed" with evil spirits or demons. The Old Testament speaks to the subject in Deuteronomy 28:28: "the Lord will smite you with madness and blindness and confusion of mind if you disobey his commandments . . ." In the first century the ancient Greeks and Romans wrote about "mania" using descriptions that were different from those describing other human problems of the day, such as mental retardation. During the Renaissance period of the fifteenth and sixteenth centuries, doctors started to keep better records of mental illness, although schizophrenia, per se, was not described well enough to be recognized for certain.

The first descriptions of mental illness that we can be sure matched the disease schizophrenia appeared about 200 years ago, at the beginning of the nineteenth century. In those days it was called insanity, not schizophrenia. Historians have found that delusions, hallucinations, and lack of emotion were cited as symptoms to describe certain patient behavior of that era. These descriptions are similar to schizophrenia as we know it today.

More stories and reports about "insanity" during the mid-1800s appear to describe what today is called schizophrenia. At the beginning of the 1900s doctors were calling this type of mental illness *dementia praecox*, which means "mad, or out of one's mind." Finally, in the year 1911, a German physician renamed it *schizophrenia* because of the splitting of thought processes that he saw. The name has stuck and is used worldwide today, although considerable abuse and misuse of the word continues.

The number of people afflicted with mental illness

greatly increased after 1800. Whether this is because of improved diagnosis and record keeping, or whether there actually has been an alarming increase in the incidence of schizophrenia, is often debated. Whatever the explanation, the recorded growth in all categories of mental illness over the past 200 years is astonishing. The U.S. census began identifying the "insane and idiotic" for the first time in 1840. The number of mental institutions (called insane asylums) increased dramatically. By the year 1900, about one out of every hundred persons in our society was being diagnosed with schizophrenia. This number remains steady even today, nearly a century later.

Most human diseases occur unevenly around the world. Diseases like cholera, typhoid fever, and dental cavities all depend to some extent on factors like living standards, sanitation, and diet. Some other diseases, such as cancer, do not seem to follow any pattern at all. Schizophrenia also fails to follow any specific pattern, and because it is also complex to diagnose as a disease, the compilation of statistics is difficult. Using present observation and data-collection methods, it is simply not clear today whether the incidence of schizophrenia is stable or increasing.

Schizophrenia occurs in people between the ages of fifteen and fifty-five for the most part. In the United States it affects about one in every hundred persons at some point in their lives. In other countries, these numbers vary. In Western Ireland, for example, schizophrenia affects one out of every twenty-five people. Schizophrenia occurs in both men and women about equally everywhere. However, it generally occurs at younger ages in males than in females.

Schizophrenia affects individuals in the lowest social class more often than any other socioeconomic class. Poor economic and social conditions evidently increase the incidence of schizophrenia. One theory says that because the lower classes tend to have more economic stress and hardship than the higher social classes, more cases of schizophrenia occur there.[3] Another theory, known as the social-drift theory, suggests that because of the confusion caused by the disease, many victims lose their jobs, and with fewer options, soon "drift" downward into the lowest social class, where they are then counted as having schizophrenia.[4]

Is Schizophrenia A Disease Of 'Civilization'?

Does progression from "uncivilized" to "civilized" conditions in the modern world affect the incidence of schizophrenia in a society? Changes in work, family, marriage, and living conditions may add new pressures that less advanced societies did not have to worry about. There is some evidence that 'civilization' is responsible for many of the health problems we see today, but there is simply not enough evidence to prove or disprove this factor as a cause of schizophrenia.

Studies during the past thirty years have examined the incidence of schizophrenia (and other diseases) in places like New Guinea, India, Ghana, and Taiwan. Most of the studies show that in societies having almost no contact with modern civilization, schizophrenia is rare. As these societies increase their contact with modern cultures, the amount of schizophrenia increases.[5] Thus, schizophrenia does appear to be a disease of civilization to some extent. Factors such as attack by viruses, changes in diet, social stresses, and environmental hazards such as pollution might be some of the effects of civilization that increase the incidence of schizophrenia, perhaps by somehow altering the chemistry of the human brain. Much more research is needed to produce more reliable conclusions.

3

What
Characterizes
Schizophrenia?

In everyday life, most people are capable of having lots of fun at play, getting things accomplished at work, and sometimes even doing things that may be considered weird or bizarre. But for the most part, normal people talk and act and think in a pretty ordinary, conventional, and well-organized manner.

A person who has schizophrenia is not always immediately recognizable, but the person is usually talking or behaving strangely. In diagnosing schizophrenia, it is important to first try to eliminate, or rule out, other problems the person might have. Many other kinds of conditions might look like schizophrenia but in fact are not. A person who is "high" on drugs, particularly stimulants, may appear to have symptoms similar to those of schizophrenia. Some forms of mental retardation often have symptoms similar to those of schizophrenia. Mental retardation, of course, has nothing to do with schizophrenia. It is a completely different problem, in which poor development or damage to the brain has caused impaired intelligence. Mental retardation is not a mental illness.

Schizophrenia Does *not* Mean "Split Personality"

Many people think that the term *schizophrenia* means split personality. It does not. Persons with schizophrenia do not act like two (or more) separate personalities, or switch their personalities from one to the other. Where, then, did this myth come from?

The word **schizophrenia** comes from the Greek *schizin,* meaning "split" and *-phren,* meaning "mind." Over many years, these root words have been misinterpreted to distort the meaning of the word schizophrenia. The split- or multiple-personality idea is one of those distorted meanings.

Schizophrenia is best thought of as a disorder in which the mind is separated from reality. People with schizophrenia escape (or split off) from reality and retreat into their own private worlds of fantasy. Although the root words for the term Schizophrenia do mean "split mind," the "split" pertains to a breaking up of the mental functions, not the personality. The three major parts of a person's mind—thinking, feeling, and acting—are not working as a team. We say they have "split from reality." This is what schizophrenia is all about.

There is, indeed, a mental disorder known as "split personality," clinically known as multiple personality disorder. This is a separate, and actually less serious mental disorder, *not* related to schizophrenia. The book *The Three Faces of Eve,* by Corbett Thigpen, depicts an individual who displays the rare multiple personality disorder.

Schizophrenia is a psychosis, and a psychosis is any form of mental illness that is so severe that a person is no longer capable of telling what is real. Such people are usually incapable of getting along in society by themselves (see Fig. 2). One of the first things done in diagnosing schizophrenia, is to test for reality.

People who can cope in the real world can tell the difference between what is part of themselves and what is not a part of their body or mind. But how do the confused thinking and the illusions of make-believe people and places in the mind of a person with schizophrenia affect their "reality?"

Figure 2. Reported rank order of symptoms noted in at least 50 percent of schizophrenic patients before hospitalization.*	
Symptoms	%
Tense and nervous	80.4
Eating less	71.7
Trouble concentrating	69.6
Trouble sleeping	67.4
Enjoying things less	65.2
Restlessness	63.0
Can't remember things	63.0
Depression	60.9
Preoccupied	59.6
Seeing friends less	59.6
Feeling laughed at	59.6
Loss of interest	56.5
More religious thinking	54.3
Feeling bad for no reason	54.3
Feeling too excited	52.2
Hearing voices/seeing things	50.0

*Source: American Journal of Psychiatry 137: 801–807.

When a person's thoughts and feelings get really mixed up, they have hallucinations and delusions. Hallucinations are truly imaginary sensations, but very real to the person who has them. For example, a person might "see" animals in a room that aren't really there. Or they might "feel" bugs crawling under their skin. Delusions are false beliefs. Some people with schizophrenia believe that they themselves are dead. Others believe they are some famous or dead person, like Jesus Christ, or the Queen of England. They aren't with us in the real world. Their "reality testing" has gone haywire.

There can be many symptoms of schizophrenia. Some researchers believe that schizophrenia is not a single disturbance at all. Instead, they think that it may be a mixture of multiple disorders of brain functioning. Other professionals think that we have only scratched the surface in our understanding of schizophrenia. Some day we may classify and treat schizophrenia in a completely different way.

These ideas will become more clear when causes and treatments are discussed in a later chapter. For now, let's look at a case study of a real individual with schizophrenia.

A.J.—A Case Study[1]

A.J. was always extremely shy. As a small child, he would run away and hide when visitors came to the house. He had one or two boy friends but as a teenager he never associated with girls. He did not enjoy school parties or social functions.

He had few interests and did not engage in sports. His school record was average, and he left high school at the end of only two years. The principal felt that he "could have done better." He also remarked about A.J.'s "queer" and seclusive behavior.

Shortly before leaving school, A.J.'s shyness increased greatly. He expressed fears that he was different from other boys. He complained that the other children called him names. He became untidy, refusing to wash or wear clean clothes.

After leaving school, A.J. worked at a number of odd jobs. He did not always show up for work when he was supposed to. He never held any one job longer than a few weeks. Finally, no one would hire him, and he stayed home.

He became more and more seclusive and withdrawn from community and family life. He would sit with his head bowed most of the time and refused to eat with his family. When visitors came, he would hide under the bed. Eventually, he refused to take a bath or get a haircut.

A.J. occasionally made "strange" remarks. He frequently covered his face with his hands because he felt he looked "funny."

The boy was interviewed by a doctor when he was brought to a mental health clinic at age seventeen. At that time A.J. was making strange faces. He had a silly smile that he used inappropriately. A young man of average intelligence, he knew who he was and where he was, but he could only answer questions in a "flat" tone of voice. He complained of having the same thoughts in his mind over and over.

A.J. was admitted to a state hospital with a diagnosis of schizophrenia. Further tests showed many other symptoms of the disease.

It is important to note that A.J.'s symptoms of schizophrenia did not occur overnight. The symptoms most often develop in a slow, gradual process. Poor relationships with other people and withdrawal from social contacts are usually early symptoms.

Persons with another kind of schizophrenia, paranoid schizophrenia, have delusions or "fantasy beliefs." Often they believe themselves to be some great historical figure. At other times they may be utterly convinced that people are "out to get them," to do them harm in some way. Paranoid behavior is a delusion that reflects distrust or suspicion. The following case is an example.

One such person with paranoid schizophrenia was L.K., a patient in a state mental hospital. L.K. believed that he had made the greatest discoveries in the history of man. Such beliefs are called delusions of a grand nature. He also thought that people had been "after him" for more than thirty years. Such ideas are called paranoid-type delusions. L.K. "heard" the evil people chasing him by way of powerful "radio voices." These beliefs are called hallucinations.[2]

Expressions Of Schizophrenia In Writing And Drawing

Actions alone do not always give the best clues for determining whether a person has schizophrenia. It is often easier to see how the person compares with normal persons in the performance of certain tasks, such as writing. The following letter, written by an eighteen-year-old girl, reveals the confused and frightened state of her mind.

Dear Dad: Please come to see me immediately. It's very urgent that I see you as quickly as possible. Just now my insides are rotting with each meal I have to eat with very disagreeable old hags. But it's a matter of life or death & if I don't get any response from you as yet I haven't, I swear by that Bible I jump in front of a car. That's how in need of fun I am Goddam it. Come up as soon as possible. Here are the Fatal Day and the one Red Letter day, is the one that I'll do it on when released. Last chance! Danger. I'll be a corpse on 16th of the month when I'm out. Goodbye forever, Helen R.[3]

Another example is a printed postcard sent by a person with schizophrenia. To get the idea of the writer's thoughts and feelings, try reading the postcard out loud. Then try to explain what it says.

To: *The football department and its members present & future, The University of New Mexico, Albuquerque, N.M.*

I depend on correct, honest supplementation of this card by telepathy as a thing which will make clear the meaning of this card. There exists a Playing of The Great Things, the correct, the constructive, world or universe politics, out-in-the-open telepathy, etc. According to the Great Things this playing is the most feasible thing of all; but it is held from newspaper advertising and correct, honest public world recognition, its next step, by telepathic forces (it seems), physical dangers, and lack of money. Over 10,000 cards and letters on this subject have been sent to prominent groups and persons all over the world. Correct, honest contact with the honest, out-in-the-open world. This line of thought, talk, etc., rule. The plain and frank. Strangers. The Great Things and opposites idea. References: In the telepathic world the correct playings. Please save this card for a history record since it is rare and important for history.[4]

The point is clear. These writings show thoughts and feelings that are abnormally distorted. That is, we can't make head or tail of what the disturbed people are trying to say. The writing expresses the thoughts, emotions, and actions of individuals who have schizophrenia. This method of diagnosis is not used alone, however. It simply adds to the information already gathered about the person, and helps to confirm the diagnosis.

Mentally ill persons often express themselves through pictures. Just as researchers have collected much information about the behavior and speech of persons with schizophrenia, many have likewise cataloged drawings and paintings from afflicted persons.

Other Visual Aids To Diagnosis

Pictures and drawings are used in other ways to aid the diagnosis of mental illness. In one such testing method, the patient is shown pictures and asked for thoughts or responses to each. Such methods may draw from the patient's thoughts and feelings that might not otherwise be revealed. Providing the opportunity for an individual to respond openly about what he or she "sees" can give important clues to the professional about the person's thought processes and state of mind.

The Rorschach (pronounced roar-shock) inkblot test is another test of that sort. The images used are random "blobs" of ink. They have no deliberate meaning, and are completely open to one's individual interpretation and imagination.

The same inkblot images have been used over and over with many different patients throughout the world. As a result, responses from thousands and thousands of individuals to the same "pictures" have been collected. This data has allowed mental health professionals to catalog "normal" responses, as well as the abnormal responses from persons with schizophrenia and other mental illness.

The inkblots are presented to the patient with a simple question, such as, "What do you see in this picture?" When the patient responds, he or she may be asked to explain more fully: "Tell me more about it." There are no right or wrong answers because the pictures are arbitrary, meaningless inkblots made by chance. However, normal people will respond that they see ordinary things, such as people, animals, mountains, flowers, and so on. Mentally ill people will report that they see bizarre scenes, conflicts, events, strange beasts, or make-believe objects from their fantasy world.

How Does Schizophrenia Feel?

The experience of having schizophrenia is both scary and exhausting. How do we know? Most individuals with schizophrenia have periods in their lives when their symptoms disappear, or when treatment has put their schizophrenia to rest for a while. During these periods of remission, they are able to share their experiences. Researchers have collected vast amounts of information from individuals with schizophrenia about what it's like. Hearing about schizophrenia from their perspective can help us to understand how it feels to suffer from the disease.

Therapists who deal with patients report that most persons with schizophrenia complain about a nagging feeling of being "phony" or unreal. Most normal people from time to time have periods when they feel a bit false, as if they are playing a role. Being polite on a lousy date, or pretending to be unconcerned about a promotion or a new job may serve to keep our personal lives on an emotional level that we can handle at a given time. As a defense against processing too many distasteful emotions, human beings often hide how they really feel by pretending that everything is "just fine" when it really is not. In fact, what keeps us flexible human beings, able to change our roles from light-hearted to serious, or from hard-working to lazy, is largely dependent on how we feel about ourselves. Most normal people have a good feeling about who they are. This feeling of self often helps us to get through a day filled with many problems and many different things to do.

Schizophrenia distorts, even destroys this important

concept of self. These individuals cannot shift gears quickly in life, or keep straight just who they are, how they should act, or what they should feel at the right time. Work, play, love, hate, frowns, and smiles are all mixed up inside the person. Therapists who work with such patients have ascertained that being in such a predicament must feel pretty awful inside.

When a person feels unreal, other things in their daily lives get jumbled up, too. Religion and faith often become additional confusing issues to deal with for the person with schizophrenia. Such issues are abstract enough for normal people to contend with, but for some mentally ill persons, they can be a nightmare. Mental patients may become fanatics who quote scary passages from the Bible or rant and rave about religious doctrines, or other issues they seem to believe are important.

Persons with schizophrenia may be quite confused about what it means to be a man or woman. They are never sure how well their performance compares with the "normals" of society. Usually, they withdraw from the real world, and operate deeper in their own inner fantasy world, which seems safer from the confusion they suffer.

Normal people can look at themselves to some extent and understand their own behavior. In people with schizophrenia, that useful "feedback" mechanism that helps us act as humans is blocked. It's all part of the same picture: feeling, thinking, acting are all garbled and distorted in schizophrenia. At its worst, many patients report that their body and their actions don't feel the same. This is a dilemma endured by persons with schizophrenia that is indeed difficult to understand.

People with schizophrenia usually tell of feeling very "empty" and worthless. Feelings are a very human trait. If feelings are somehow blocked, the person may feel nonhuman on the inside, and likewise appear, often, to be nonhuman from the outside as well. Some sufferers of schizophrenia are so separated from their own feelings that they get the idea that they are no longer human. Imagine what it must be like for a sufferer of schizophrenia to constantly think of himself or herself as a bad, incompetent, or worthless person. Even worse, imagine how confusing and painful it must be to think of oneself as not a person at all.

Maintaining a close relationship with another person is obviously difficult amid all this confusion. Such a state of constant agitation also greatly reduces the concentration that one needs to work at a job. People with schizophrenia often fail in their marriages and careers after a short time.

Many, "normal" people have what is called a poor self image or poor "self-concept." That is, they don't feel very good about themselves sometimes. These feelings can be very painful but the feelings schizophrenia brings are usually far worse than this. Some patients report to their therapists feeling completely enslaved and dominated by debilitating feelings of doom. Those feelings are considerably beyond the level of such feelings held occasionally by most individuals who lead normal lives.

4

What Causes Schizophrenia?

The causes of schizophrenia are still a mystery. Years of scientific research provide no solid explanations, but many different theories that represent the many ways in which scientists have attempted to explain the cause. The diversity of the theories also shows why the disease is so complicated.

It may seem hard to believe that in a world with so much knowledge and technology that no one has figured out what causes schizophrenia. But we do not understand everything about how human beings function. This is especially true about the mental processes of humans. Although we can repair or replace many malfunctioning organs in the human body, most mechanisms of the brain remain out of reach of our understanding so far. There is perhaps some irony in the fact that the human brain is the very organ which sets us apart from the other animals, yet we haven't yet figured out how it really works!

Scientists have certainly tried to figure it out, however, and they work very hard on the problem. Through years of experiments some pretty good ideas have been thought out and tested. Present thinking focuses on three or four theories of what causes schizophrenia:

1. The *Genetic Theory* proposes that schizophrenia is inherited, passed down through the genes from generation to generation.

2. The *Interpersonal* (*or Environmental*) *Theory* suggests that schizophrenia is caused by the pressures of living in the world and interacting with family members and others.

3. The *Biochemical Theory* suggests that alterations in normal body chemistry produce the abnormal thinking, feeling, and behavior characteristic of schizophrenia.

4. The *Bio-Psycho-Social Theory* proposes that schizophrenia is caused by a combination of some or all of the factors named above.

There are dozens more theories, but these four are the ones that have been given the most study. It is important to understand that all of them are only theories. All are plausible, all are shown by some evidence to be true, but the effects of each, and the exact cause of schizophrenia is not known. A closer look at these four major theories is in order.

The Genetic Model

The Genetic theory offers an explanation of schizophrenia based on the hereditary materials which make up each of our cells. Genes are pieces of the strands of chemicals which make up the *chromosomes*. These chromosomes are the components of each cell in the body that are responsible for determining the characteristics which make us who we are. Genes are the mechanism by which characteristics are passed on to the next generation. Some scientists propose that people with schizophrenia have *different* hereditary materials in their bodies than do people without schizophrenia, and that they pass the genes for the disease down to their children through reproduction. This does not mean, however, that every person who ends up with schizophrenia must have had parents who were also mentally ill.

Researchers have studied and argued about this idea for years. One way to study this has been to observe twins. Identical twins have the same genetic makeup, according to the rules of heredity and biology. If one twin has schizophrenia, but the other twin does not, it would mean genes cannot be the sole cause, and other factors must be involved. On the other hand, if twins raised in different families or in different environments both end up with schizophrenia, it would mean that inheritance may be a cause or a strong contributor.

Twins are comparatively rare in the general population, and twins with schizophrenia are even more uncommon. However, scientists have studied all the twins they can find. Their research is fascinating and complicated, but the question is still unsettled. For example, sometimes both twins in a family are afflicted with schizophrenia, but not as often as needed to prove that genes are responsible for the disease. It is true that there are genetic components in members of the same family that can make them have similar physical and mental characteristics. Most researchers think that similarities in physical makeup—chemicals in the body— between blood relatives may make it more likely for schizophrenia to occur, but they are yet not sure how this happens.

Mental illness does, unfortunately, run in families. Records show that the sons and daughters of a parent with schizophrenia have more of a chance of getting the disease than do children of parents without schizophrenia. One likely reason for this may be genes. On the other hand, records also show that up to 75 percent of children who have one parent with schizophrenia are mentally sound.[1] Still other studies show that if a child has one parent with schizophrenia, he or she has about one chance in ten of getting schizophrenia.[2] For now, it seems safe to say that the tendency to get schizophrenia does seem to be inherited.

But if schizophrenia happens more in family groups, does this mean it is due primarily to genetic material? What about the effect on children raised in a home where excess stress exists because a parent has schizophrenia?

The Interpersonal Or Environmental Model

A lot of young people might like to blame life at home with their parents as the cause of problems or maladjustments of many kinds, including serious ones like schizophrenia. In some cases such an accusation may be reasonable.

Can one's environment, or experiences, or family really cause schizophrenia? Does *stress* cause schizophrenia? Or does having the wrong genetic factors or chemistry in your cells *allow* stress to make a person a better target for schizophrenia? For now, the only possible answer is "perhaps." The effects of environment and family circumstances on the incidence of schizophrenia are being studied all the time. The answers to these questions may one day win the Nobel Prize in medicine for someone.

The Biochemical
Model

The functions of our minds and bodies depend upon the continuous action of electrical and chemical processes. The brain is part of the body's nervous system. It has billions of nerve fibers. When a stimulus—a noise or a light or a smell, for example—acts upon a nerve ending at one of the sensory organs such as eyes, ears, or nose, the information is then carried as an electrical impulse, or signal, to the brain. Complicated chemical and electrical processes translate the message and allow it to provide us with information. Simple examples are: The wood stove is hot, the music is loud, the knife cut is painful. More complex examples are: That girl or boy is nice (pleasure). That is so funny (laughter). That makes me very sad (tears).

The nerve fiber connecting a big toe to the brain is not like a solid wire or a continuous piece of thread. There are spaces where nerve fibers meet others and signals are passed from one to another on their way to the brain. These spaces, called *synapses* (sin-APP-sees), are filled with tiny amounts of chemicals. For the electrical signal to jump across the spaces, perhaps switch to another track, and continue its journey to the brain, the chemicals must change from one side of the gap to the other.

The chemicals involved in such biological processes are called *neurotransmitters*. The amount and type of chemicals at the synapses control the transmission of information. From extensive research, it is known that when those chemicals are not right, or get mixed up in some way, the transmission of signals goes haywire, affecting the way the brain reads the signals it receives. When a signal is scrambled because of chemical changes, the brain may interpret the information wrongly, perhaps even in an inappropriate or bizarre fashion. The reason these chemical changes occur is not known, but many scientists believe that these alterations of normal body chemistry produce the characteristic abnormal thinking and feelings of schizophrenia.

One of the most studied chemical neurotransmitters is called *dopamine* (DO-pah-mean). In research on the biochemical theory, scientists have tried to learn whether persons with schizophrenia have more brain dopamine than normal people.

Measuring the amount of dopamine or any other drug in the brain or in the synapses between nerve endings is no easy task. One way of investigating the effects of dopamine is to give large doses of *amphetamines* (am-fet-uh-means) to animals and, under carefully controlled conditions, to humans. Amphetamines are a class of drug which actually puts extra amounts of dopamine in the brain. The results of such research are interesting. Even small increases of these chemicals in the brain cause a person to have delusions and hallucinations. Laboratory animals that have been given large doses have been observed to act like persons with catatonic schizophrenia; their behavior is bizarre—they may stand in one position, or pace endlessly.

Research has thus shown that excessive amounts of brain dopamine produce behavior which resembles schizophrenia. Other neurotransmitters are now also being investigated. It cannot be said definitely yet that schizophrenia has a biochemical cause. It *can* be said that biochemistry seems to play an important role in schizophrenia and other mental illness.

The result of research on these three theories is clear: *Schizophrenia cannot be said to be caused by a single factor.* Most recent research leans toward the biochemical explanation as the most likely cause. The evidence so far suggests that before anyone can get schizophrenia, his or her body must use up some of the existing chemicals in its cells. Then, for whatever reason, the body makes new chemicals which are abnormal and harmful, thereby causing schizophrenia. Such harmful changes have not been found to occur in the body chemistry of normal persons. Why the body chemistry of certain people goes "out of order" is not yet known.

The Bio-Psycho-Social Theory

Some researchers suggest that even with biochemical abnormalities, certain other events still must occur to cause schizophrenia, and that such triggering events may be found in thought processes, or perhaps in social or environmental conditions. If this theory eventually proves correct, studying the causes of schizophrenia will become a much more complicated and time-consuming process.

Some social scientists try to explain the causes of schizophrenia entirely without factoring in any chemical or biological influences. Mental disorders are explained as a consequence of human motivations, drives, and unconscious forces. These theories suggest that people can become overstressed or overloaded with information and stimulation, and lose the ability to cope with their resulting anxiety and apprehension. They reason that a sort of "psychological circuit breaker" pops. When that happens, the individual's mind and behavior sometimes seeks refuge in a fantasy world. Often individuals return to an earlier stage of life, perhaps infancy, and behave accordingly. This behavior appears as schizophrenia.

Of the myriad of opinions and ideas that have tried to explain schizophrenia over the past fifty years, most have some merit. Few, however, have yet been researched with suitable scientific rigor to contribute major evidence that there is a single cause of schizophrenia. Nor has any indication been found as to just how multiple causes might be intertwined.

Treating Schizophrenia

Schizophrenia is an illness. Like other diseases, it can be treated. However, it is different from the majority of medical diseases, because it cannot, at present be cured. The disturbed mind of a person with schizophrenia is not well enough understood yet to provide a true cure. Nevertheless, research on and experience with the disease constantly improves our understanding. Some quite effective treatments are available today.

How Was Schizophrenia Treated In The Past?

Before mental illness was really understood, people tried a variety of imaginative cures, which today seem downright cruel. There were some rather desperate attempts to help mental patients get rid of their illness. For example, some mental patients had holes bored in their skulls to "release the evil spirits." Others were chained to a wall to control their behavior and curb their self-destructiveness. Still others were whirled in a harness suspended from the ceiling. Such methods were used in one insane asylum 400 years ago. Most such "treatments", of course, had no effect and accomplished nothing!

In the nineteenth century, people with schizophrenia were usually confined to mental hospitals. There, professionals did what they could to help, but the outcome was not always good. Patients who were completely out of control were confined to padded cells or restrained in some way to keep them from hurting themselves or others.

In *electroconvulsive therapy,* a low-voltage electric current is passed through the brain. This "shock" produces convulsions in the patient. The patient is first put to sleep with an anesthetic, so there is no feeling or memory of the shock, and the treatment is not painful. Just what this procedure does to the brain is not well understood, but it sometimes gives relief from the symptoms of mental illness. It is most effective on patients with mental illness involving depression.

Shock treatment, as it was often called, was invented in 1938, and was sometimes used on patients with schizophrenia. However, it has not proved to be as effective as medication. It is seldom used to treat schizophrenia today.

A method of brain surgery which permanently disconnects several sections of the brain is known as *psychosurgery*. Some symptoms of severe schizophrenia, such as hallucinations and delusions, could be lessened by this procedure. However, other symptoms, such as withdrawal and feeling alone, were not altered. This drastic surgery was usually only done for extreme, chronic cases after all other treatments had failed. The medical term for this rather drastic operation is *frontal lobotomy*. Today this operation is almost never used, mainly because the results of psychotropic medication for schizophrenia are far more successful.

Who Treats Schizophrenia?

Patients receive much more personal care today. *Therapy* is another word professionals use when they talk about treating sick people. There are many types of professionals who may be involved in providing therapy to persons with schizophrenia and other mental illnesses. Among them are psychologists, psychiatrists, social workers, nurses, nutritionists, and other therapists and counselors.

There is an important difference between psychologists and psychiatrists, both in their training and in the therapy they provide. *Psychologists* are trained in the science of human behavior. They study all aspects of human behavior, from intelligence to emotions, from early childhood to old age. They test and diagnose psychological disorders, as well as help people with their problems. Most practicing psychologists spend between six and ten years studying and training at colleges, universities, and various mental health facilities.

Psychiatrists, on the other hand, are trained physicians who have specialized in mental disorders. After four years of college, they attend medical school, where they study general medicine for another four years. Then they specialize in psychiatry for four or five more years. Psychiatry is simply the branch of medicine which deals with mental disorders. Because they are medical doctors, they can treat the physiological aspects of mental illness, and administer drugs as part of therapy to control mental illness. Many psychiatrists also do "talking therapy," known as psychotherapy, which will be covered later in this chapter.

Social workers first train for four years in college, and then attend three additional years of postgraduate school, where they have supervised clinical work and special training in handling all aspects of people's problems. Social workers focus on evaluating individuals and families to provide a treatment program that usually includes several disciplines. By communicating with patients, families, and other professionals, they provide a critical link between treatment facility and home care for patients.

Nurses, nutritionists, and other professionals who have a minimum of four years of college training in their respective fields, also help to treat schizophrenia. They provide assistance in their own fields, but many have special knowledge in areas such as in mental illness, education, rehabilitation, or special diet therapy.

Chemical Therapy

Modern science has greatly increased the help available to people with schizophrenia. Chemistry alone has made tremendous advances. In the 1950s various medications effective for schizophrenia were discovered accidentally, while treating other ailments. Research on drugs to control the symptoms of schizophrenia blossomed, and a dozen or more are now used to treat the disease.

The most successful treatment by far now is medication (Fig. 3). It is generally called *antipsychotic* medication. This literally means "against psychosis," and some of the drugs are used to treat other mental illness besides schizophrenia.

Drugs have the effect of slowing down jumbled thinking, and quieting the feelings of the individuals. By doing so, such medications help individuals with schizophrenia to bring their own feelings and thinking back to reality, and their behavior back into control. Today more than two dozen such drugs are available for treating schizophrenia.

Figure 3. Types of Antipsychotic Drugs

Type	Generic Name	Trade (Brand) Names
Aliphatic phenothiazines	chlorpromazine	Thorazine, Largactil, and others
	triflupromazine	Vesprin
Piperidine phenothiazines	thioridazine	Mellaril
	mesoridazine	Serentil
Piperazine phenothiazines	fluphenazine	Prolixin, Permitil
	trifluoperazine	Stelazine and others
	perphenazine	Trilafon, Phenazine
	prochlorperazine	Compazine
	acetophenazine	Tindal
Thioxanthines	thiothixene	Navane
	chlorprothixene	Taractan
Butyrophenones	haloperidol	Haldol
	pimozide	Orap
	droperidol	Inapsine
Dibenzoxa-zepines	loxapine	Loxitane, Daxolin
Dihydro-indolones	molindone	Moban

Medications used as antipsychotic drugs are also called *psychotropic* drugs. Exactly how and why these substances work is not entirely known. We learned earlier that certain chemicals are responsible for carrying the messages between different nerve receptors within the brain. Psychotropic drugs are known to change the chemicals in the brain in ways that slow down and calm the activity level, and bring the brain back to more normal functioning. The person feels more relaxed, less afraid, and concentrates better.

Not all persons with schizophrenia respond to drugs, but most do. The best drug for a patient is often found by "trial and error". While drug therapy is a far cry from the treatment of even fifty years ago, much more information about an individual's chemistry, as yet unavailable, is needed to be able to predict, in advance, which medicine will be most effective.

Side effects are a minor problem with psychotropic medicines. Some, but not many, patients experience allergic reactions such as skin problems or even blood disorders, to these medicines. Others get muscle problems, or the shakes, or gain weight. While these are annoying problems, the overall benefit of the drugs is usually greater than the inconveniences.

Treatment of schizophrenia with drugs has kept many sufferers out of hospitals for long periods of time. Many patients still need some time in a hospital. But the majority of persons with schizophrenia today do not spend their lives, or even long periods of time, in a hospital.

Another type of chemical therapy used in the treatment of schizophrenia is vitamin therapy. As noted earlier, chemicals called neurotransmitters are responsible for carrying messages to and within the brain. Some researchers believe that in people with schizophrenia some of these chemicals have been changed to poisons or toxins, and that these new toxic chemicals are the cause of hallucinations. Some studies seem to show that certain vitamins actually block the poisons from being made. Most recently, vitamin B_{12}, known as niacin, has been found to do this. The information is too new to be well understood. Such measures are therefore used with caution.

Vitamins have been a fad treatment for many ailments in recent years. Until researchers really have a good understanding of what value, if any, the use of vitamins has in treating schizophrenia, their use must be considered experimental at best. This does not mean that vitamins should be ignored. Every individual needs to insure that his or her body has a healthy supply of all vitamins, through food or supplements.

Psychotherapy

Psychotherapy is treatment designed to alter mental responses rather than to make physical changes in the body. To do this, trained professionals use suggestion, re-education, reassurance, support, and persuasion to help a person modify their thinking and emotions. Sometimes special techniques such as hypnosis or psychoanalysis are also used to help the individual deal with problems that are difficult to understand or even to identify.

Psychotherapy is absolutely necessary along with medication. Medication often helps to control the more serious behavior such as delusions and hallucinations, but it does little for helping a patient understand and deal with various aspects of their illness, such as their emotions, self-esteem, confidence, and their techniques for getting along with people. Therefore, the two types of treatment are almost always used simultaneously.

When a person with schizophrenia is given psychotherapy, the professional who treats him or her must be very supportive. That is, the therapist spends many hours helping the patient to understand what has happened to him or her. New ways of explaining and dealing with the world are explored and taught to the disturbed person. A trusting friendship between the therapist and the patient is important for constructive changes to take place.

One-on-one individual psychotherapy is time-consuming and quite expensive. Often patients enter into *group psychotherapy*. Here they are able to work on their problems in a small group of people who have similar problems. One leader, a psychotherapist of some sort, helps steer the therapy sessions with activities, by making suggestions and observations, or sometimes by giving advice. Such group treatments are less expensive and often as good if not better than individual therapy.

It is often a great relief for people suffering from mental illness just to learn that they are not alone with their problems, and to have the help of others in dealing with them. Group activities, vocational training programs, and old-fashioned recreation programs also help patients learn to handle many of the things they never learned how to do because of their schizophrenia. Again, this kind of program is most effective when used along with psychotropic medicine to control the schizophrenia. Both are essential parts of a total treatment package.

The Role Of The Family

Any chronic illness tends to have terrible effects upon the patient's family. Many people become confused and angry at what has happened to one of their family members. Most feel a lot of guilt about schizophrenia because of their fear that they may have somehow inadvertently caused the illness. In her novel *I Never Promised You a Rose Garden*, H. Green has written a passage that expresses very well how families feel. The patient's mother, speaking with the doctor for the first time, says:

> *You see—all these days. . . . all these days we've been thinking and thinking how and why this*

could have happened. She was so much loved! They tell me that these illnesses are caused by a person's past and childhood. So all these days we've been thinking about the past. I've looked, and Jacob has looked, and the whole family has thought and wondered, and after all of it we just can't see any reason for it. It's without a cause, you see, and that's what's so frightening.[1]

Schizophrenia is truly tragic to families. But since this passage was written, the use of psychotropic medicine has made possible astounding improvements in treatment. No longer do family members necessarily face long periods of hospitalization, as more patients become capable of functioning on an outpatient basis. Families are now encouraged to be part of the treatment. Most individuals diagnosed with schizophrenia are encouraged to remain in contact and build needed trust with family members. Relatives can help by learning to cope with some of the difficult behavior. They must provide the patient with support and understanding. They must learn to be therapists of sorts themselves.

Guilt is a horrible feeling. A father may feel that his child could have avoided schizophrenia if only he had spent more time at home. A mother may feel that occasionally losing her temper with a child may have helped to cause the schizophrenia. Some professionals unfortunately heap even more guilt on parents.

Feeling personal guilt or laying guilt on someone else for a patient's schizophrenia is truly wasted energy. To blame family conduct as a major cause for schizophrenia is not really fair. Families do not cause schizophrenia simply by mistreating their children. As we've already seen, parents may pass along genes that make their children more susceptible to schizophrenia, but this could hardly be called intentional.

All families have stresses, conflicts, and difficult,

emotional times. But a great number of people from very disturbed families do *not* develop schizophrenia, nor is it proven whether schizophrenia results even partially as a result of stress or family disharmony.

The problems that family members face in dealing with schizophrenia include recognizing and dealing with the many symptoms of the illness. The victim of schizophrenia usually withdraws from friends, family, and fellow workers. That is, they stop participating in daily routine activities, and spend more time alone with their thoughts and feelings. Dealing with this withdrawal is very frustrating for family members. Hallucinations and delusions are downright embarrassing to relatives when these symptoms appear in front of others. There is always the possibility of aggressive behavior. Occasionally the patient may become violent.

Another worry is suicide and accidental death. The rate of suicide among persons with schizophrenia is twelve times higher than that for the general population.[2] For some patients, disturbed thinking includes self-mutilation or suicide gestures. Sometimes "voices" instruct patients to sit on railroad tracks, or cease to eat, or jump off bridges. Suicide resulting from such hallucinatory experiences most often occurs in the most agitated patients. Other patients may believe they have special powers—that they can fly or walk on water. Such beliefs are risky to the patient's health and longevity if he or she acts on them. Finally, despair is often a major part of schizophrenia even during recovery stages. Some patients, envisioning a lifetime of suffering, or realizing that their personal goals have been jeopardized, decide to take their own lives.

Families that successfully cope with schizophrenia contribute a lot to the overall treatment and recovery possibilities. The important concept is that recovery from schizophrenia depends on how well the individual can learn to cope in his or her environment. If those around the ill person set realistic goals and expectations, progress will usually be good. If, for example, social stimulation and relationships are made available, but not pushed on the individual, the response will probably be better.

Schizophrenia does not just happen overnight. Nor does it disappear overnight. Like diabetes, schizophrenia is a chronic disease. It can usually be controlled with proper care. For diabetes the control and treatment is diet, exercise, and for some, insulin. For schizophrenia, the control and treatment may include any or all of the types of medication and psychotherapy that has been discussed.

Another way of looking at control versus cure is to realize that alcoholism is never cured either. But thousands of people every year learn to cope with their disease by not drinking anymore and by addressing other needs in their lives. You might say that they still have alcoholism, but for now, they are in remission. If a person with diabetes stops taking insulin or forgets her schedule of diet and exercise, she will get very sick. If a person with alcoholism stops getting the support from others he needs, he might start drinking again. Likewise, certain events in one's life may trigger the symptoms of schizophrenia. Sometimes the disease can be mild, sometimes harsh. It may last for a few days or a lifetime. It may come and go at various times. Who actually recovers from schizophrenia, and who does not is a difficult but often-asked question, and is examined in the next chapter. The variations of schizophrenia add to both its mystery and the complexities of its treatment.

Encountering Someone With Schizophrenia

Approximately one out of every hundred people in the world has schizophrenia. It is, by far, the world's most serious mental illness. Thus, it is likely that at some point you will know someone—a neighbor, friend, schoolmate, or relative—who suffers from schizophrenia. The number of people with schizophrenia worldwide is approximately 50 million.

In dealing with strangers, it is always best to be cautious. Being polite, of course, is always a safe way to treat *anyone* you meet on the streets, on a subway, or a bus, or in a store. As a rule, the vast majority of mentally ill persons are not considered dangerous. They are more often withdrawn and frightened. They may not even know you are around because they are very much in their own world. They are "out of reality." But the truth is that the public is probably in less danger from mental patients, as a group, than from what appear to be mentally "normal" people in our world today.

A person who is acting strangely may not have schizophrenia at all. He or she may be under the influence of alcohol, drugs, or both. Then again, they might be suffering from a combination of alcohol, drugs, *and* schizophrenia, a common problem today.

If you find it necessary or desirable to carry on a conversation with someone you suspect is a little "out of it," you must remember that all people can really be treated the same. If questions or statements from an individual don't make sense, you can always respond with what is called "reflective feelings" statements.

Reflective listening involves careful listening first. Then, the speaker's words are carefully stated again, so that the meaning is not changed. The process of restating the words spoken, is a way of showing "I care enough to hear what you said."

This polite process for accepting a person without threatening or challenging will usually keep the conversation quiet and calm. Here is a brief example of how an interaction with a person who has schizophrenia might go:

Abnormal person on the street: *The whole world is in my pocket. My fingernails talk to me and tell me that. Green slime, can't get it out of there. Night time crawls around. World in pocket, world in pocket.*

You: *I guess you feel like the whole world is in your pocket today, is that right?*

Person: *Oh, yeah, been there twenty-five years. I'm the boss, I keep it in my pocket. Don't let it out, EVER. Fingernails tell me to. Green slime ball.*

You: *Your fingernails tell you to never let the world out of your pocket?*

Person: *Can't let it out, I own the slime ball. Might crawl right away, then where would it be?*

You: *I guess you're afraid that it might crawl away.*

Person: *Crawl away, slime ball, in my pocket. See ya, bud.*

This fictional conversation is *typical* of one you might have. Do you see the listening and "reflecting" of the person's feelings or ideas? This is the same way professionals work with the mentally ill. You accept their fantasy world. (You couldn't talk them out of it if you tried.) You acknowledge their world for a few minutes, but without, of course, getting involved yourself. This does not harm either the ill person or you. Most importantly, it allows the person with schizophrenia to keep his or her self-respect. In this process, the person is not made fun of, and not threatened. That would be unkind, perhaps even unsafe, because the person with schizophrenia is already very insecure and mixed up.

On the other hand, here is an example of something you should NOT say, as it would be neither kind nor a good idea to do so:

You: *What's this garbage about a stupid green slime ball world in your pocket? And fingernails don't talk to people. You know that's not possible. That's crazy talk and you ought to cut it out.*

This kind of approach to a mentally ill person is unlikely to do any good, and might even anger an individual to the point of emotional reaction or even violence. Certainly it would show poor manners and lack of respect for a person who, at least for the moment, cannot be held responsible for his or her behavior.

Furthermore, because schizophrenia displays many complicated symptoms, it is not always possible to tell whether an individual is in the normal world, completely in their own abnormal world, or perhaps somewhere in between. Complete strangers or others whom you sense are possibly not mentally sound should always be treated with kindness and understanding.

6

Two Case Studies
of
Schizophrenia

Because treatment is far from an exact science, the question of why certain individuals respond to either medication or psychotherapy, or both, still baffles professionals. But the growing number of individuals who *do* respond is cause for optimism. Many persons who at one time would have been hospitalized for life are now able to lead reasonably normal lives, work, and raise families.

Two case histories, based on actual patient experiences with professionals, help to answer, by example, the two questions: Who recovers? Who does not? The first case study is an individual named John. Despite incredible hard work by all the professionals and his family, John still suffers terribly from most aspects of schizophrenia. In contrast, there's Sam, a shining example of someone who has schizophrenia, but is able to lead a normal, productive life.

This woman with catatonic schizophrenia might remain motionless in her bizarre posture for hours.

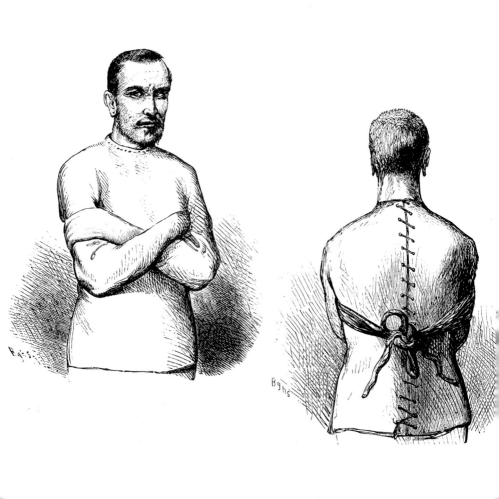

*Three views of how schizophrenics were treated in the
nineteenth century. Above: front and back view of man
in a straitjacket. Top facing page: a "lunatic's chariot"
drawn by mental patients chained together. Bottom facing page:
the "crib," a device used to restrain unmanageable cases
in a New York institution.*

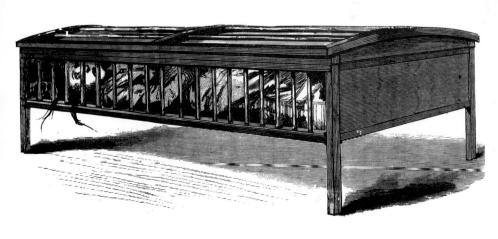

Among the odder nineteenth-century treatments for mental illness was this "suspensory" technique used at the Salpêtrière Hospital in Paris.

An inkblot like the ones used in the famous Rorschach test. This test, named after Swiss psychiatrist Hermann Rorschach (1884–1922), elicits a subject's responses to such inkblots. These responses can aid in the diagnosis of certain mental disorders.

A homeless schizophrenic whose condition has been worsened by alcohol. The increase in homelessness in our nation has made schizophrenia a highly conspicuous social issue.

Family members of a person with schizophrenia talk to
a therapist. Mental health professionals consider family
to be an important aspect of a patient's treatment. They can
lend essential support and understanding.

INSIDE TWO MENTAL HOSPITALS

The pages that follow are a photo portfolio by photographer Mary Ellen Mark that take you inside two mental institutions. One is in the United States and the other in China. The first is the women's security ward (Ward 81) of the Oregon State Hospital. The women there are considered dangerous to themselves or to others. Karen Folger Jacobs, a writer and social scientist who accompanied Mark during a thirty-six-day sojourn on the ward during the mid-1970s, writes, "Bodies slump just a shade more than you've ever seen bodies slump before. Flesh seems to respond more to gravity than to muscle and bone."

Mark also visited the Second Mental Hospital of Chongqing in Ditlo, China in 1989. There she found a philosophy of treatment very different from what she had seen in the United States: "In the United States the emphasis is often on punishment, but here doctors seemed almost amused by the craziness. If someone was acting really psychotic, nurses and patients alike would laugh along. There seemed to be no underlying threat of punishment. It's impossible to take pictures that make a mental hospital look glamorous, but the atmosphere at Chongqing was very open."

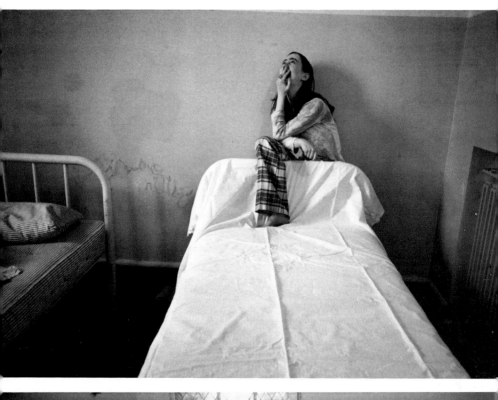

Three photos from Ward 81, Oregon State Hospital.
Facing page top, "Woman crying behind bed";
Facing page bottom, "Suzie making faces in bed";
Above, "Women dancing to music"

Ward 81, Oregon State Hospital.
Above, "Mona and Beth taking a shower";
Facing page top, "Feet strapped down in bed";
Facing page bottom, "Woman after shock treatment"

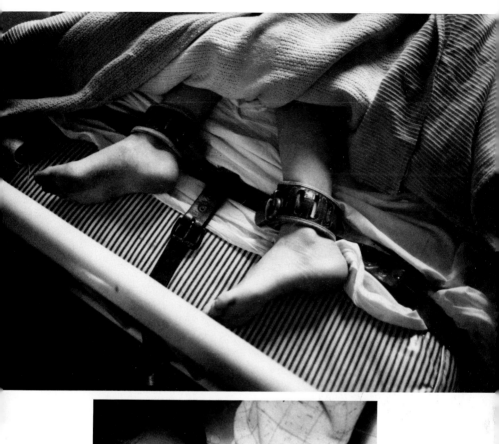

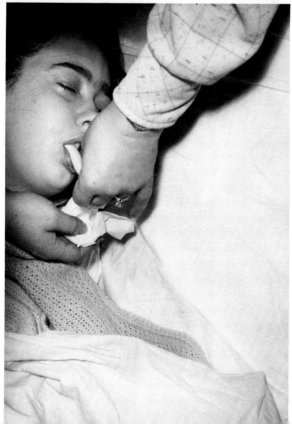

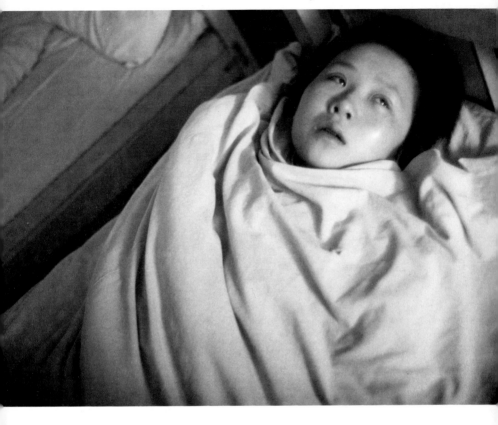

*Three photos from the Second Mental Hospital of Chongqing,
Ditlo, China. Above, "Woman in Bed Portrait";
Facing page top, "Patients Wearing Pajamas";
Facing page bottom, "Patient Undergoing Shock Treatment"*

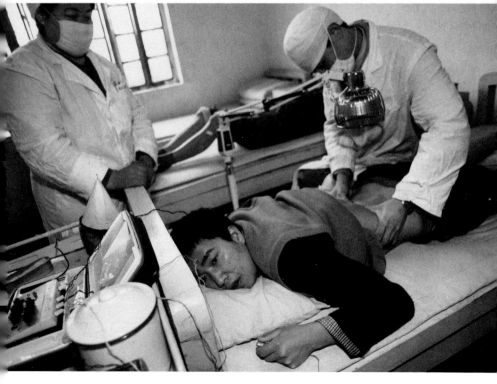

Ward 81, Oregon State Hospital:
"Mary Looking Out Window"

John: A Case With A Poor Outcome

It's always hard to know what actually took place in someone's childhood. However, everything that is known about John reveals that he had always been a bit different, peculiar, and odd. All his relatives agree that he had never really been a member of the family. John rarely showed any enthusiasm for family activities. He spent most of his childhood being quiet and withdrawn.

Being a member of his family was difficult for him. His mother was always "going away" on "family trips." At about the time he was in the fifth grade, he overheard a group of neighborhood children talking about his mother and her being in the hospital because she was crazy. At about the same time, John noticed that his mind seemed to be floating out of his body to a quiet place. This frightened him at first. But then, this special magical power became more and more comforting. It provided a safe place to which he could retreat.

School was fine as long as John did not feel pressured. If he was rushed, as during a test, he often had to reread each question carefully and slowly. If he tried to hurry, all the letters or numbers began to stand out as individual elements. Words lost their usual meanings and became strings of unrelated letters. The other students never really gave John trouble; they just tended to ignore him. The few times John tried to break in, to become a part of the group, his attempts failed. He never did gain acceptance by peers. The few people John knew were also social outcasts.

School always seemed to demand performance, but home was a refuge. John's mother had never really had any authority, and his father had chosen long ago to do the chores they originally had tried to give John. It was so much easier to take out the garbage or do the dishes than to watch John perform these tasks at an infuriatingly slow pace. Thus, John never assumed the youthful responsibilities that lay the groundwork for later participation in the social system outside the family. The feelings of oddness, not belonging, and worthlessness were merely gnawing at the edge of John's consciousness. He continued in this suspended state until high school, when increased demands for social and academic skills made him feel more withdrawn and less capable than ever before.

No single dramatic event, family problem, or personal tragedy was the cause of John's failure to mature socially. It was clear, however, that being a member of a group, belonging to anything or anyone, was simply not to be for him. John became the person who, in gym class, always turned right when everyone else turned left. He ate alone at a small corner of a large cafeteria table. He made people laugh when he tried to be serious, and was taken seriously when joking. John found it hard to concentrate and much more pleasant to use the magic of escape.

John's withdrawal from reality had become more elaborate over the years. His fantasy world was now inhabited by superhumans who spoke a special language, the significance of which was known only to John. This powerful, make-believe world held increasingly more meaning for him than the world of school and family. Although physically present both at home and at school, John spent less and less time with teachers, students, and family.

Without anyone really noticing, John stepped over the boundary from the world of external social interaction into that of the imagination. He had tried out this new world bit by bit over the years, then one day simply had not returned. It was some time before his family noticed that John now not only failed in his responsibilities to the family, but also in those to himself. Not doing little jobs around the house was tolerable, but not washing for weeks without being reminded was unacceptable. They tried to reason, cajole, push, and beg John to show some concern for his personal hygiene. Finally, when they could take it no longer, they called the hospital. John was sixteen at the time.

John was in and out of the hospital six times during the next ten years. At first there had been much hope. Both therapists and family felt John could be cured, to return home functioning at a higher level than he had attained before hospitalization. Indeed, for a brief period their goals for him seemed within reach. Medication helped John to concentrate. Occupational, recreational, group, and individual therapies were focused on teaching him skills he had never learned. Discharged in remission, John returned home. Soon, however, he began taking less care of himself, experienced the old feelings of worthlessness and loneliness, and eventually gave in to the call of his fantasy world. He returned to the hospital, worse off for having failed the first "cure."

With each succeeding admission, discharge, and readmission, John lost a little more self-confidence and the strength to try living outside the hospital. Over the years, John's family tired of the burden of having to care for their adult child. The pain, frustration, anger, and guilt they felt after one of his visits home was too much to bear. They still had much of their own lives to lead.

Today, John shuttles back and forth between the state hospital and a community halfway house, where the old family conflicts are replayed. The halfway house members are tolerant of John until he requires close, constant supervision. Then, John is sent to the hospital. Treated, then released, he may continue in this way until the halfway house refuses to accept his return. If that happens, John could become a permanent resident of a state psychiatric hospital or perhaps manage to survive by himself on the edge of society.[1]

Sam: A Case With A Good Outcome

It is unlikely that anyone would have predicted that Sam would one day be hospitalized, diagnosed, and treated for schizophrenia. There is nothing unusual in Sam's background that one could point to as a predictor of his future episode with schizophrenia.

His family was, from all indications, stable and supportive. His parents got married in their early twenties. After working for several years, his mother assumed primary reponsibility for rearing their first child. His father, meanwhile, directed much of his energy toward establishing himself in a local company.

Sam was the second of three children. Healthy as an infant, he grew into a lively, engaging child, enthusiastically taking part in frequent family outings. His parents expected Sam (as well as their other children) to take on a share of the family chores as he grew older. Although he grumbled, as children frequently will, Sam usually finished his chores on time.

He did well throughout school, generally bringing home A's and B's at report-card time. Liked by both teachers and peers, Sam had a circle of friends who always did things together. Although one or two children were always moving into or out of the group, Sam maintained close contact with this core group of friends.

In high school, Sam began discovering new areas of interest and seemed to enjoy the expanding network of social and academic relationships. Emerging as a leader in school, Sam was chosen as editor of the school paper during his senior year. He took the job quite seriously and spent many hours writing stories, editing, and planning the layout of the paper. A perfectionist in his work, he would revise and reorganize an issue until it was just right.

During this time, Sam's social life had also widened to include both casual and serious relationships. In contrast, his home life seemed to be one of frequent conflict, as is true between most adolescents—seeking to establish their identities—and their parents. However, under the friction and Sam's testing of parental limits, a warm stability maintained the family.

Toward the end of his senior year, Sam began making plans to attend a large college well known for its journalism department. After a summer of work, play, and anticipation, he went away to school. At first, Sam was a little homesick. The work was harder than in high school, and he found it more difficult to meet people. Although Sam occasionally worried about this, college life was too hectic to allow much time for self-pity. Overall, he seemed to be adjusting as well as anyone, until the first exam period.

Although Sam studied diligently, he failed the first exam. Since he had never failed an exam before, the F did not seem real. Over the next few days, Sam found it harder and harder to concentrate. He began to believe that college was society's attempt to brainwash its young people by forcing them to think alike, and that it used grades to reinforce this conformity. It became clear to him that the school was keeping a detailed record of his activities because those in authority realized his potential power to overthrow the system.

He stopped studying and began burning all his notebooks and records so that they would have no written evidence of his work. Sam also started keeping irregular hours so that no one could follow his movements, thereby avoiding any traps. He began cooking his own meals. In every issue of the college paper, he found more coded and symbolic evidence that the school authorities considered him to be a major threat to their plans. On more than one occasion, he thought that he decoded a message transmitted during a local radio show.

In an attempt to alert others, Sam tried to describe the brainwashing plot to his friends. Although he was not always well received, he continued dodging the traps of the school authorities and talking to others. He became very excited and began making plans for exposing the school's plot. This might have gone on for some time had Sam not shown up at a local television station demanding free time to broadcast a general warning about public education. When denied, Sam became very angry, threw furniture, and eventually had to be subdued by the police.

Referred for psychiatric evaluation by the court, Sam spent several weeks in a psychiatric hospital. Treated first with medication, he finally calmed down. Since Sam could not recall the events preceding hospitalization, it was necessary to rely on family and friends to provide an explanation of what had happened. After several months of outpatient therapy, he was able to return to school.

Even now, Sam occasionally has fleeting moments when he wonders if the school authorities really were out to get him. However, these periods have been quite brief. Accepting any sort of failure still is a problem for Sam, though he has learned what to expect of himself during periods of stress. Whenever he feels he has failed to perform adequately, he experiences the old thoughts that others are plotting against him. He has learned, however, to arrange much of his life so that he can avoid too much unexpected stress. Overall, Sam has used his psychotic experience to learn something about himself and to cope more effectively with life's unexpected setbacks. Since he knows that failing is so stressful for him, he has lowered his expectations somewhat to ensure more frequent success. He has decided to accept the assurance of lower-level success in place of the chance of bigger victories but potentially bigger losses.[2]

7
Schizophrenia: Past, Present and Future

In the past, research on schizophrenia was focused mainly on discovering the cause or causes of the disease. At present, most research is concerned with the abnormal biochemical aspects. In the future, it appears, scientists will try to find specific genes related to either symptoms or causes of schizophrenia. The final years of this century may reveal new information about these genes, that will change forever the way we treat, and perhaps, prevent schizophrenia.

Genetic Research

The likelihood that schizophrenia is inherited, made most evident by research on twins, suggests that genes may carry a predisposition toward the disease. Like diabetes and hypertension, schizophrenia tends to run in families.

Psychotropic medicines made startling improvements in most patients with schizophrenia starting only about thirty-five years ago, and scientists continue to determine how these drugs work on our body's unique programming chemistry—our genes. Genetic research is the focus of the future.

Researchers believe that a single gene could not account for schizophrenia. Instead, they believe the tendency to contract schizophrenia must arise from a number of genes acting together. Everyone probably has some degree of biological vulnerability, or propensity, to schizophrenia. Thus, if certain unfavorable genes become active, the disease may start. Similarly, an unfamiliar gene produced by the body may increase a person's susceptibility to acquire an illness like schizophrenia. With increased susceptibility, other factors such as stress, body-chemistry changes, diet, or perhaps other agents, may then trigger onset of the disease. Only further advances in genetic research will determine whether specific genes that cause schizophrenia can be identified. In fact, this type of discovery has already taken place for other diseases.

It has become possible to isolate "culprit" genes. Cystic fibrosis, which strikes one in every 2,500 Caucasians, is a disease that produces excess secretions of mucus from several organs including the lungs. This disease can cause death from a blockage of the digestive tract and other complications by age four or five. Sickle-cell anemia strikes one in 500 black children born in America. The disease causes changes of an individual's red blood cells, making them unable to function properly in the body. Both diseases are genetic.

Locating the specific genes which cause these two life-threatening illnesses was a true milestone of medical science. Some genetic disorders can now be detected at birth by simple tests, which are now routinely performed in many hospitals. One such screening program is for the genetically inherited disorder called phenylketonuria

(PKU), which occurs in about one in every 15,000 births. The gene causing PKU prevents children with the disease from properly breaking down the amino acid phenylalanine, which consequently causes toxic levels to accumulate in the blood. Mental retardation is the result. By detecting this genetic deficiency in a newborn, this toxic reaction and the resulting mental retardation can be prevented with a special diet that allows normal development. Unfortunately, very few such genetic disorders are treatable at the present time.

Finding and isolating the particular gene that causes a major health disorder is only half the battle. Unless the faulty gene can be altered so that each cell will duplicate and send the correct information throughout the body, the disease caused by the error will continue.

If schizophrenia becomes traceable to a single defective gene, it is theoretically possible to replace or supplement the defective gene with a good, "normal" gene. A set of techniques for taking genes from different sources and combining the pieces of DNA (deoxyribonucleic acid—the chemical that genes are made of) in a "corrected order" outside the body is called *recombinant DNA technology*. In a fascinating and very complex process, DNA can be transformed in certain bacteria, from a defective unit to a genetically correct or "fixed" unit. Once the transformed genetic material is produced, it must somehow be re-delivered into the afflicted person, to turn the illness around or stop it cold. Science is not quite there yet, but it is the hope and dreams of both patients and researchers everywhere.

The Treatment Of Schizophrenia: Yesterday, Today, Tomorrow And One Hundred Years From Now!!

Let's use a fictitious woman—we'll call her Janet—to look at how schizophrenia was treated in the past and at present, and how it might be handled in the future. From the knowledge of present-day research, we can project what it may be like to have schizophrenia in another fifty years, and finally one hundred years from now.[1]

Janet in 1932. *Janet, age twenty-four, was brought to the hospital by her father. She had been withdrawn, isolated, and strange since age eighteen. She was kept at home with her parents. They were very embarrassed and uncomfortable about a family member labeled as mentally ill. Then Janet's mother died, and her father couldn't care for her, the other children, and work also. The hospital has bars on the windows. It is dark, impersonal, and spooky. Her father was told that Janet is very ill and must stay for a long time.*

Every month, Janet's father visits her, but he comes alone so as not to frighten the other children with the atmosphere of the hospital. Janet is dressed in a hospital gown, sits and stares most of the time. Other patients pace, yell, or make strange sounds. The place stinks, too. Sometimes staff speaks with her, but because they usually get no response, they go away. After a while, they only talk to her when they want her to go to bed or come for meals.

Soon after admission to the hospital, she had what is called "insulin shock therapy." They gave her insulin until she had a seizure. This treatment had worked for some patients, but did nothing for Janet. The doctor told her father that there was nothing else he could do. But Janet might recover spontaneously. Some patients did.

Janet does not recover. Her behavior worsens because of the hospital environment. Her original symptoms remain the same. She stops taking care of herself. She no longer brushes her teeth or combs her hair. What little respect she had fades away.

Finally, after two years, her father stops visiting Janet. She is left alone.

Janet in 1992. *Janet, age 19, has been brought to the hospital by her parents. Although she has been withdrawn, seclusive, and eccentric for about a year, it was not until her refusal to look for work, or even to leave the house, after high school graduation, that her parents became frightened enough to seek help. Their family physician has suggested that Janet be treated in a hospital.*

The hospital is in a beautiful spot. Many people sit outside, reading or talking. It is not in the least bit apparent which of the people are patients and which are visitors or staff members. The walls inside are decorated with paintings, some done by former patients. There is a snack bar, a reading room, a music room, and a television and video center. Only one hallway is locked.

The hospital psychiatrist tells Janet's parents that she feels that Janet will need to stay maybe a couple of weeks at most. She introduces them to the psychiatric social worker, who helps them plan for regular visiting by the whole family, and how to deal with this at home when she soon comes home. Janet is expected to wear her own clothes, and to wash them herself in the available machines. She will also help out, as will all the patients, in the kitchen sometimes and with other jobs that need doing. It feels more like a summer camp than a hospital.

Her parents visit at least twice a week, and when they can, her brother and sister also come along, and they go down to the lake for a picnic. They also meet weekly with the social worker to discuss Janet's progress and to talk about what they ought to expect from her.

Janet's treatment program has many parts: medication, regular meetings with her therapist, group activities, and individualized training. A user-friendly computer is also used each day to help her learn some personal and vocational skills, like typing, for example.

In just a few days, after trying some different medicine and doses, Janet is much less withdrawn. She talks to her family about everyday events, although she does complain about some of the medication's side effects. After a week, her odd behaviors, such as talking out loud when no one is there, are almost gone. She's still unsure about how to make friends, and what sort of a job she should get, or how her life will go for her. Though uncomfortable about the medication, she agrees to continue to take it when she goes home.

After only ten days, Janet returns home. She enrolls in a secretarial training program funded by the State Vocational Rehabilitation Office. During her studies she lives at home, but does not participate in many activities outside of school.

A month before graduation, she stops taking her medication. Before she can even look for work, her symptoms come back. She is taken back to the hospital. With a full therapy program once again, she is ready for discharge into the world again after two weeks. This time, she is referred to an outpatient young people's group for continued support. Through this group she makes new friends. In time, she even decides to share an apartment with one of her new friends, but she keeps close ties with her family, also.

Ten years later, Janet continues to take a very small dose of medication each day and remains well. She works as a clerk-typist and as a library volunteer in the hospital where she was treated.

She is still somewhat withdrawn and never goes out with men. She has not gone to college as her parents had once hoped. But she appears comfortable with her quiet, structured life.

Janet in 2042. Janet, age 14, is brought to the mental health center by her parents. Since there is a family history of schizophrenia, her parents had been told many years ago of the possibility that they might have a child who would develop schizophrenia. They were educated about the warning signals that might alert them to its presence. Having seen some of these signals, Janet's tendency to daydream, lapses of attention, moodiness, they have decided to have her checked.

A series of medical tests and computer analyses confirms the diagnosis of schizophrenia and pinpoints the site and nature of the physiological disturbance. A wide array of medications have been developed in the past fifty years, each of which controls a different type of schizophrenia. One of these improved treatments is just right for Janet. A computer helps with the selection. A monthly injection will remove the symptoms with few side effects. Additional therapy is not even necessary.

Janet is enrolled in a class offered by the mental health center, which teaches persons with schizophrenia and their families about the illness, its treatment, and what they can do to ensure complete recovery. The family is encouraged to return if, under stress, Janet begins to experience any symptoms.

For the next few years, Janet makes her parents' life difficult, as do her teenage brother and sister. She has the usual adolescent rebellion, sometimes trying to use her illness as an excuse for all sorts of special privileges she wants. She and her brother argue over whose treatment hurts worse, her schizophrenia injection or his allergy shot. Her life has its ups and downs, to be sure, but she is not significantly impaired in her ability to adjust to them.

Janet in 2092. *Janet is twenty-one years old. She has just graduated from college and is about to begin a career in journalism. When she was born, Janet was screened, as are all newborns, for the presence of an abnormal protein, which if undetected, may produce symptoms of schizophrenia later in life. Only about one in about every 1000 babies are found to carry this protein during routine screenings. The chances of having this abnormal protein, which could develop into schizophrenia, is much less than, say fifty or one hundred years ago, because the new techniques of replacing or fixing defective proteins has greatly eliminated them from being passed on to the next generation.*

Janet was treated with a medication which neutralizes the protein, turning it into a harmless substance which is then excreted through the urine. She has never experienced any symptoms of schizophrenia, and never will. Nor will her children likely be found to carry this abnormal protein.

If the crystal ball is right, schizophrenia as we know it today will hardly exist in another hundred years. Meantime, two and half million[3] individuals with schizophrenia live in this nation alone. Worldwide, the figure exceeds a staggering 50 million.

You have taken a major first step in the battle against schizophrenia: *education.* The term should no longer be just a hard-to-pronounce word shrouded in mystery. Schizophrenia is a disease that must be assaulted with the same energies with which we now combat cancer, diabetes, and heart disease. Many debilitating disorders have already been conquered by science. Professionals and researchers are battling schizophrenia, too. One day, they will win.

Organizations to Contact for Further Information

American Medical Association
535 North Dearborn Street
Chicago, IL 60610
(312) 464-5000
Contact: Tom Carroll
Purpose: Membership organization of physicians; disseminates scientific information to members and the public.

American Psychiatric Association
1700 18th Street NW
Washington, D.C. 20009
(202) 797-4950
Assistant Director: Ron McMillen
Purpose: Professional organization of psychiatrists whose purpose is to study the nature, treatment, and prevention of mental disorders.

American Psychological Association
1200 17th St. NW
Washington, D.C. 20036
(202) 955-7600

Canadian Schizophrenia Foundation
2231 Broad Street
Regina, Saskatchewan, Canada S4) 1Y7
(306) 527-7969
General Director: I.J. Kahan

National Alliance for the Mentally Ill
1-800-800 NAMI
Purpose: Alliance of self-help/advocacy groups concerned with severe and chronic mentally ill individuals. Seeks to provide emotional support and practical guidance to families.

The Psychology Society
100 Beekman Street
New York, NY 10038
(212) 285-1872
Director: Pierre C. Haber

Source Notes

Chapter 2: Schizophrenia: A Mental Illness in Perspective

1. *Diagnostic and Statistical Manual of Mental Disorders,* 3d edit., revised. American Psychiatric Association, Washington, D.C. 1987.
2. World Health Organization. "Report of the International Pilot Study of Schizophrenia," Geneva, Switzerland, WHO, 1973.
3. E. Fuller Torrey, M.D. *Schizophrenia and Civilization,* Jason Aronson, New York, 1980, 84.
4. Ibid. p. 173.
5. Ibid. p. 43–76.

Chapter 3: What Characterizes Schizophrenia?

1. Adapted from A.I. Rabin, (1947) "A case history of a simple schizophrenic." in Burton, A., and Harris, R.E. (eds.) *Case histories in clinical and abnormal*

Psychology, New York: Harper and Row, also found in *Introduction to Psychology,* 5th Edition by Hilgard, E.R., Atkinson, R.C., and Atkinson, R.L. Harcourt Brace Jovanovich, New York, 1971.

2. Adapted from R.W. White, *The abnormal personality.* New York: The Ronald Press, 1956, as found in Holland, Morris K. *Psychology: An Introduction to Human Behavior,* D.C. Health & Company, Lexington, MA, 1974, p. 174.

3. Lewinson, T.S. "Dynamic disturbances in the handwriting of psychotics; with reference to schizophrenic, paranoid, and manic-depressive psychoses." Reprinted from *The American Journal of Psychiatry,* volume 97, pages 102–135, 1940, as found in Coleman, James C. & Broen, William E., *Abnormal Psychology and Modern Life,* Scott, Foresman & Company, Glenview, IL, 1972, p. 299.

4. Ibid. p. 299.

Chapter 4: What Causes Schizophrenia?

1. John S. Strauss and William T. Carpenter, *Schizophrenia.* (New York: Plenum, 1981.)

2. Don D. Jackson, *The Etiology of Schizophrenia.* (New York: Basic Books, Inc., 1960.)

Chapter 5: Treating Schizophrenia

1. H. Green, *I Never Promised You a Rose Garden.* (New York: Signet Books, 1964.)

2. A.D. Pokorny, "Suicide rates in various psychiatric disorders." *Journal of Nervous and Mental Disease,* 1964, 139, pp. 499–506.

Chapter 6: Two Case Studies of Schizophrenia?

1. Adapted from: Kayla F. Bernheim, and Richard R.J. Lewine, *Schizophrenia: Symptoms, Causes, Treatments.*

(New York: W.W. Norton & Company, 1979), page 185.
2. Ibid. p. 188

Chapter 7: Schizophrenia: Past, Present, and Future

1. We gratefully acknowledge W.W. Norton & Company, for their permission to reprint selected excerpts from *Schizophrenia: Symptoms, Causes, Treatments,* by Kayla F. Bernheim and Richard R.J. Lewine.

Glossary

The definitions in this glossary pertain mainly to their use in this book. More general definitions can be found in psychology textbooks or unabridged dictionaries.

amino acid—a chemical compound containing carbon, which is an essential component of protein molecules in the body.

antipsychotic medication—see psychotropic medication.

bell curve—see distribution curve.

biochemical—chemistry pertaining to living organisms and especially the vital processes of life.

biochemical model—a model or structure that can be used to test ideas dealing with the chemistry of living organisms.

bio-psycho-social model—a model or structure which proposes that the cause of schizophrenia comes from three disciplines: biology, psychology, and sociology.

catatonic schizophrenia—a form of schizophrenia that is often marked with alternating periods of excitement and stupor (mental confusion, daze).

chromosome—a DNA-containing body of the nuclei of a cell in plants and animals that determines and transmits hereditary characteristics.

chronic disease—any disease which progresses slowly and persists over a long period of time; often a disease without a permanent cure.

cystic fibrosis—an inherited disease of mucous glands throughout the body, usually developing during childhood which causes pancreatic insufficiency and pulmonary disorders.

dementia praecox—a premature and irreversible deterioration of intellectual faculties with accompanying emotional disturbance resulting from brain disease. See schizophrenia.

disorganized schizophrenia—one of the types of schizophrenia in which the patient is incoherent, and exhibits grossly disorganized behavior. He or she may also exhibit grimaces, withdrawal, and other odd behavior.

distribution curve (bell curve)—a graphic display of statistical data that shows events according to the number of times they occur.

dopamine—a chemical compound produced in the body.

DNA—Deoxyribonucleic acid. A complex molecule with a double-stranded, helical shape, which is the principal component of human genes, and determines to a large extent our inherited characteristics.

DSM-III-R—Diagnostic and Statistical Manual of Mental Disorders, Third Edition-Revised is the official publication of The American Psychiatric Association, Washington, D.C., 1987.

electric (electro) shock therapy—a shock produced by application of a small electric current through the brain.

feedback mechanism—the brain's system that shows us the results of our behavior.

flat emotion—feelings which are dull, colorless, or bland.

frontal lobotomy—a brain operation that severs nerve tracks in a portion of the brain in an attempt to relieve certain severe mental illness.

gene—within each cell, the biologic carrier of heredity; genes are self-reproducing and located in definite positions on particular chromosomes.

genetic model—a model or structure that explains a phenomenon using the science of heredity.

genetics—the scientific study of heredity.

hallucination—a sense perception not founded upon objective reality.

hebephrenic schizophrenia—a type of schizophrenia in which the victim displays foolish mannerisms, delusions, hallucinations, and regressive behavior.

heredity—the genetic transmission of characteristics from parents to offspring.

hypnosis—an artificially induced sleeplike state in which an individual is extremely responsive to suggestions and commands made by the hypnotist.

inkblot drawings—a meaningless ink pattern, made by folding on itself a paper containing a spill of ink. The unusual patterns thus produced are used in the Rorschach Inkblot Test.

insane asylum—an archaic term for an institution for the care of the mentally ill.

insanity (insane)—the nonmedical, legal term for permanent mental disorder that may make a person a danger to self and others.

International Classification System—the system of categorizing mental diseases used by the world community. The DSM was developed and used primarily by the American mental health sector, but there is considerable overlap and commonality with ICD nomenclature.

maladaptive behavior—behavior which is detrimental to the individual or the group.

mania—wild or violent insanity; specifically, the manic phase of a manic-depressive psychosis, characterized by excessive excitement, exaggeration, and activity.

mental disorder—any irregularity, disturbance, or interruption of the normal mental functions.

mental illness—old term for mental disorder, but now used to mean any psychosis.

mental retardation (mental deficiency)—below normal intelligence, usually meaning an IQ below 68.

multiple personality—type of mental disorder in which the person appears to have two or more distinct personalities.

neurosis—any of various functional disorders of the mind or emotions that do not have an obvious physical cause, and which involve anxiety, phobia, or other abnormal symptoms. Also called "psychoneurosis."

neurotransmitters—the chemical messengers which carry nerve information across the gap (synapse) connecting two or more nerves in the body.

niacin—one of the B vitamins, also called nicotinic acid.

paranoid schizophrenia—the type of schizophrenia that features systematized delusions or auditory hallucinations related to a single theme. Patients can also show anxiety, anger, argumentativeness, and violence.

phenylalanine—a natural amino acid that occurs as an ingredient of many proteins in the body.

phenylketonuria (PKU)—an inherited faulty metabolism of phenylalanine (a naturally occurring amino acid in the body). It is often associated with mental defects.

predisposition—the likelihood that an individual will develop certain symptoms under given stress conditions.

protein—any of a group of complex organic compounds that contain amino acids as their basic units and occur in all living matter. Proteins are essential for the growth and repair of animal tissue.

psychiatrist—a medical doctor who specializes in the diagnosis and treatment of mental disorders and mental illness.

psychiatry—the field of medicine concerned with treating mental disorders and mental illness.

psychologist—a person trained to psychologically assess people's behavior and perform therapy, or research on such matters.

psychology—the science of mental processes and human behavior.

psychosurgery—brain surgery used to treat mental disorders or mental illness.

psychotherapy—the treatment of mental, emotional, and nervous disorders.

psychotropic medicine—any drug that has an effect upon the mind; a medication that can modify mental activity.

reflective feelings—process by which a therapist, through close listening, senses a meaning the patient is trying to express. The therapist then puts this meaning into words in order to help clarify the emotional meanings for the patient.

remission—marked improvement in the course of an illness which may or may not be permanent.

recombinant DNA technology—techniques for recombining genes from different sources in the laboratory and transferring these into body cells where they grow and divide.

Rorschach test—a test for mental disorders which uses inkblot drawings, originally devised by Hermann Rorschach in 1911.

schizophrenia—the most serious psychosis form of mental illness, always marked with delusions, hallucinations, or disturbances in mood and thought patterns.

seclusive—seeking or tending toward solitude or privacy; removed from others.

self-concept—an individual's sense of his or her own identity, worth, and capabilities.

self-defeating—injurious to one's self.

self-esteem—pride in oneself, feeling of personal worth.

sickle-cell anemia—a hereditary blood disease.

side effects—effects other than the one(s) for which a drug is used.

split personality—see multiple personality.

social worker—a person trained for community work that promotes the welfare of the community and individuals through, for example, health and psychological clinics.

standards—a set of criteria commonly used and accepted as an authority.

stress—a mentally or emotionally disruptive or disquieting influence on the body.

stupor (catatonic stupor)—a condition of lethargy and unresponsiveness; mental confusion or daze often accompanying the catatonic type of schizophrenia.

symptom—any phenomenon that is a departure from normal, generally indicating disorder or disease.

synapse—the connective point between nerves, at which the nerve impulse passes across the gap by means of a chemical agent called a neurotransmitter.

theory—an organized set of assumptions about how things operate, made in an attempt to account for current observations, and to predict future ones.

therapist—a specialist in conducting therapy, such as psychotherapy.

therapy—the treatment of illness or disability. See psychotherapy.

toxic reaction—the result of a harmful, destructive, poisonous, or deadly agent.

toxin—see toxic reaction.

treatment—the application of remedies with the object of effecting a cure; therapy.

unconscious forces—a capacity of the human mind, of which a person is unaware, to affect his or her behavior.

For Further Reading

American Psychiatric Association. *Diagnostic and Statistical Manual of Mental Disorders*. 3d edit., revised. Washington, D.C., 1987.

Carson, Robert C. et al. *Abnormal Psychology and Modern Life*. Glenview, Ill.: Scott, Foresman, 1988.

Feldman, Robert S. *Understanding Psychology*. New York: McGraw-Hill, 1988.

Sheehan, Susan S. *Is There No Place on Earth for Me?* Boston: Houghton-Mifflin, 1982.

Torrey, E. Fuller. *Surviving Schizophrenia: A Family Manual*. Rev. edit. New York: Harper and Row, 1988.

Walsh, Maryellen. *Schizophrenia: Straight Talk for Families and Friends*. New York: William Morrow, 1985.

Index

Antipsychotic medication, 53–55

Biochemical theory, 43, 46–49
Bio-Psycho-Social theory, 43, 48

Case histories of schizophrenia, 11–12, 34–35, 36, 37, 64–70, 73–78
Catatonic schizophrenia, 24, 25
Causes of schizophrenia, 42–49
Characteristics of schizophrenia, 31–41

Chemical therapy, 53–56
Concept of normal distribution, 17–18
Cystic fibrosis, 72

Definition of schizophrenia, 19–25
Delusions, 20, 34, 36, 47, 59
Dementia praecox. *See* Schizophrenia
Diagnosis of schizophrenia, 21–25
Diagnostic and Statistical Manual of Mental Disorders, 21
Disorganized schizophrenia, 24, 26

Electroconvulsive therapy, 51
Environment and schizophrenia, 43, 45

Family, role of, 57–60
Frontal lobotomy, 51–53
Future treatment of schizophrenia, 78

Genetic research, 71–73
Genetic theory, 43–45
Green, H., 57

Hallucinations, 20, 34, 36, 47, 59
Heredity and schizophrenia, 43–45
History of schizophrenia, 27–30, 50–52
Human evolution, 14–15
Hypnosis, 56

Incidence of schizophrenia, 12, 26–27, 28–30, 61
I Never Promised You a Rose Garden (Green), 57
Interaction with victims of schizophrenia, 60–63
International distribution of schizophrenia, 26–27
Interpersonal theory, 43, 45

Mental illness, 9–10
Mental retardation, 31–32, 73
Multiple personality disorder, 32

Neurosis, 22–23
Normal and abnormal behavior, 11–12

Paranoid schizophrenia, 25, 26, 35–36
Phenylketonuria, 72–73
Psychoanalysis, 56
Psychosis, 22, 23, 33
Psychosurgery, 51–52
Psychotherapy, 56–57
Psychotropic drugs, 53–55

Recombinant DNA technology, 73
Rorschach test, 38–39

Schizophrenia
    case histories of, 11–12, 34–35, 36, 37, 64–70, 73–78
    causes of, 42–49
    characteristics of, 31–41
    definition of, 19–25
    diagnosis of, 21–27
    history of, 27–30, 50–52
    incidence of, 12, 26–27, 28–30, 61

treatment of, 50–63, 74–78

types of, 24–26, 35–36

Self-concept, 39–41, 48–49

Shock treatment, 51

Sickle-cell anemia, 72

Statistical analysis of abnormality, 17–18

Therapists, 52–53

Thigpen, Corbett, 32

Three Faces of Eve, The, 32

Treatment of schizophrenia, 50–63, 74–78

Types of schizophrenia, 24–26, 35–36

Visual aids to diagnosis, 38–39

Vitamin therapy, 55–56

World Health Organization, 27

About the Author

Douglas W. Smith holds a bachelor's degree in psychology from Purdue University and a master's degree in clinical psychology from the University of Wisconsin-Oshkosh. Mr. Smith is a free-lance writer who lives in South Hero, Vermont. He is married and has three children.